THE SAINT ABROAD

FOREWORD BY
RICHARD USHER

THE ADVENTURES OF THE SAINT

Enter the Saint (1930), *The Saint Closes the Case* (1930),
The Avenging Saint (1930), *Featuring the Saint* (1931),
Alias the Saint (1931), *The Saint Meets His Match* (1931),
The Saint Versus Scotland Yard (1932), *The Saint's Getaway* (1932),
The Saint and Mr Teal (1933), *The Brighter Buccaneer* (1933),
The Saint in London (1934), *The Saint Intervenes* (1934),
The Saint Goes On (1934), *The Saint in New York* (1935),
Saint Overboard (1936), *The Saint in Action* (1937),
The Saint Bids Diamonds (1937), *The Saint Plays with Fire* (1938),
Follow the Saint (1938), *The Happy Highwayman* (1939),
The Saint in Miami (1940), *The Saint Goes West* (1942),
The Saint Steps In (1943), *The Saint on Guard* (1944),
The Saint Sees It Through (1946), *Call for the Saint* (1948),
Saint Errant (1948), *The Saint in Europe* (1953),
The Saint on the Spanish Main (1955), *The Saint Around the World* (1956),
Thanks to the Saint (1957), *Señor Saint* (1958), *Saint to the Rescue* (1959),
Trust the Saint (1962), *The Saint in the Sun* (1963),
Vendetta for the Saint (1964), *The Saint on TV* (1968),
The Saint Returns (1968), *The Saint and the Fiction Makers* (1968),
The Saint Abroad (1969), *The Saint in Pursuit* (1970),
The Saint and the People Importers (1971), *Catch the Saint* (1975),
The Saint and the Hapsburg Necklace (1976), *Send for the Saint* (1977),
The Saint in Trouble (1978), *The Saint and the Templar Treasure* (1978),
Count On the Saint (1980), *Salvage for the Saint* (1983)

THE SAINT ABROAD

LESLIE CHARTERIS

SERIES EDITOR: IAN DICKERSON

THOMAS & MERCER

Text copyright © 2014 Interfund (London) Ltd.
Foreword © 2014 Richard Usher
Preface © 1969 Leslie Charteris
Publication History and Author Biography © 2014 Ian Dickerson
All rights reserved.

Published by Thomas & Mercer, Seattle

www.apub.com

ISBN-13: 9781477843000
ISBN-10: 1477843000

Cover design by David Drummond, www.salamanderhill.com

Printed in the United States of America.

PUBLISHER'S NOTE

FOREWORD TO THE NEW EDITION

The early 1980s were a glorious period for law-abiding young bookworms with "secret buccaneering dreams" to indulge themselves in the adventures of the notorious Simon Templar, alias the Saint. For one thing, there were so few distractions, no e-mail, no video games to speak of, and only four TV channels. In the UK, crisp new copies of *Count on the Saint* could be found in some branches of WH Smith, and well-thumbed paperbacks featuring the "Robin Hood of Modern Crime" could be found on the shelves of discerning second-hand bookshops. Best of all, many of the Saint's classic adventures could often be found gracing the shelves of your local public library. It was in one such public library, a dimly lit, eerily silent municipal athenaeum with strangely smoky strip lights, that I first encountered *The Saint Abroad*.

I was lucky to discover the literary Saint in the way that I did, my interest sparked by the fairly regular reruns of *Return of the Saint* on ITV, offering enough excitement to spice up even the most somnolent Sunday. This action-packed TV series, bookended by a gloriously quirky title sequence and a memorable theme tune, left an indelible impression on my boyhood imagination. So, when I discovered a series of books in my local library displaying the impeccably dressed Ian Ogilvy on their covers, it was a done deal—I handed over my library ticket and felt a tingle of excitement as the punch of ink on paper date-stamped them to my care for the next two weeks.

The Saint Abroad was one of the books ceremoniously stamped into my custody by the seemingly stereotypical librarian. I can't recall if there was a photograph of the Saint on the cover, but it didn't really matter as I began to read those marvellous adventure stories written by Leslie Charteris. I was suddenly whisked away to Paris, a place I'd only really heard about through my school geography and French lessons. "The Art Collectors"—for that was the title of the first story—brought this foreign city to life in ways that dusty old textbooks simply could not. The finer nuances of plot probably failed to register, but kidnap attempts, expensive works of art, crisp dialogue, and the odd fight scene kept my interest throughout. I so enjoyed that first literary adventure with Simon Templar that I looked forward to our next excursion in "The Persistent Patriots" even more, and I wasn't to be disappointed! There was more of that humorous Saintly dialogue, plenty of the Ungodly ripe for a bopping, and my first encounter with Simon Templar's old sparring partner, Chief Inspector Claud Eustace Teal.

A good book is sometimes a bit like that good friend you don't see very often—there is a comfort to being in their company, and you somehow fall back into your relationship and pick up where you left off, even if it's years since you were last together. That's how I sometimes feel about the Saint books, and having reread *The Saint Abroad* fairly recently, it felt like I'd enjoyed a fabulous reunion (minus the hangover and the bar bill!). If this is your first acquaintance with the book, I think you will enjoy yourself in the company of Simon Templar as he becomes embroiled in typically exciting adventures in France, the tropical African territory of Nagawiland, and foggy old London town (with a brief excursion into rural Berkshire). That said, this book is perhaps one of the more leisurely introductions you could have to the world of our "Brighter Buccaneer." *The Saint Abroad* was first published in 1969, a product of a series of collaborations attempting to adapt some of the scripts from the Roger Moore TV series into legitimate canon. The two stories featured are based upon teleplays by Michael Pertwee, adapted by Fleming Lee, and given that essential Saintly sparkle by Leslie Charteris himself. If you are a reader more familiar with the urbane characterisation conjured up by the TV Saint, you will perhaps find this a more accessible book than some of the earlier literary works. The youthful, buccaneering twentysomething Simon Templar of the formative Saint books is quite a different adventurer from the more mature and suave gentleman you will find battling art thieves in Paris, but the steely eyes still sparkle, and he still fights the good fight against the Ungodly and their fiendish plans.

—*Richard Usher*

THE SAINT ABROAD

PREFACE

Our first three experiments in turning the tables on the television producers (*The Saint on TV*, *The Saint Returns*, and *The Saint & the Fiction Makers*) having been tolerably well received, we have been encouraged to bring out yet another of these hybrid books—that is, Saint stories which were originally created expressly for television, not by me, adapted for reading as ordinary fiction by yet another writer, and indebted to me only for the parentage of the Saint himself, for sundry suggestions along the way, and for a final revision of the manuscript in which I did my best to see that the style was as close to my own as possible, short of a complete personal rewrite. In the construction of these adaptations, I have not hesitated to call for quite drastic changes from what you may have seen on the mini-screen, exactly as a film producer does not hesitate to take liberties with any story he has bought, whenever I thought I could improve on the material. In this case, reversing the traditional sequence of events, I am the character who has had the last word.

Nor do I feel that I owe any apology to old and faithful readers of the Saint Saga. The television stories which I have selected for this treatment are only those which I thought had genuine possibilities—which by no means qualifies everything that has gone out on the TV networks. Nor would I have published these adaptations if they dissatisfied me. Whether this kind of composite authorship is kosher may be debatable on a rarefied intellectual plane, but if it satisfies enough aficionados of the Saint who want more books to read than I can supply, it can't be all bad.

—Leslie Charteris (1969)

THE ART COLLECTORS

Original teleplay by Michael Pertwee

Adapted by Fleming Lee

1

"In these devaluable days," Simon Templar said, "you don't just take your money and stash it away in some nice sturdy bank, or you may very well find yourself with a nice sturdy bank full of waste paper."

"Knowing your reputation, Monsieur Templar, I can well believe that you have several bank vaults full of such waste paper," said Marcel LeGrand.

LeGrand's smile, which appeared through the thicket of his black mustache and beard like the moon seen rising through a forest, was the smile of a salesman certain that however much money his customer has at the moment, he is going to have considerably less before he leaves. The bushy-faced art dealer's hand caressed the gilded frame of one of his salon's more expensive offerings as he spoke. All around him, on walls and easels, were the colors and forms of the paintings that were his stock-in-trade. The displays were arranged so that direct sunlight could never touch the works of art, but flashes of light thrown by the passing traffic through the blue-tinted windows from the Paris street outside gave a kind of psychedelic motion to the whole interior.

"You underestimate me," Simon Templar replied with a perfect gravity. "I support the Rothschilds almost single-handed. Without my deposits, the gnomes of Zürich would have to crawl back into their caves and collect mushrooms for a living."

The Saint—the name by which the world most generally knew Simon Templar—saw no more reason to try to spike the rumors which circulated about his wealth than he saw to try to quash the legends which flourished around his reputation as a modern buccaneer, a Robin Hood whose Sherwood Forest was the world of crime in an age of industry and international finance, and whose victims were the criminals themselves. In the first place, the stories were mostly true. In the second place, efforts to refute myths tended only to have the effect of increasing belief in their validity. Thirdly, the Saint enjoyed the exaggerations, and they were useful to him. They increased the awe of potential enemies and pushed them toward elaborate precautions and nervous countermeasures which could only increase their chances of error. The same tales enhanced his powers of bluff where the police were concerned and his naturally considerable powers of attraction where women were concerned. All in all, folklore had its uses.

"I hope, then, more sincerely than ever, that you will find something here which pleases you," LeGrand said. "You will find no better selection in France—I can promise you that. And I do not think I flatter myself when I say that my judgment as to the investment value of paintings is as sound as that of any man in the world."

"No, you don't flatter yourself," the Saint said. "That is exactly why I'm here and not talking to some other dealer."

He moved slowly through the large room, whose space for hanging paintings was increased by a number of partitions jutting out across the richly carpeted floor and reaching almost to the ceiling. LeGrand followed with calculated casualness, his hands clasped behind his back.

He was a head shorter than the Saint's lean-muscled six feet two, but he made up for it on the horizontal, without actually being fat.

"Perhaps you could suggest some amount you would like to invest," LeGrand said. "I realize that taste, too, is involved, but we may as well be practical."

"*We* may as well," Simon said with a smile, "and therefore I'm not showing you my wallet until after you've shown me the price tags."

LeGrand laughed and shrugged to acknowledge his appreciation of the Saint's acumen as a bargainer. Simon noticed, looking over the art dealer's shoulder, that a tall, dark-haired man had started to step into the shop from the street, had seen through the windows that LeGrand was occupied, and had stayed outside without leaving the doorway.

"This," Simon said. "What is it?"

He had turned back to one of the framed paintings hanging on one of the partitions. Most of LeGrand's collection was pre-nineteenth century. Along this partition were some of the exceptions—contemporary productions, non-representational.

"That is chicken feathers on lacquered axle grease," LeGrand said impassively. "Interesting, no?"

"No," said the Saint. "How much do you calculate it will be worth in ten years?"

"About two francs," said LeGrand, still impassively. "Let me show you something more suitable. Something from the Renaissance—Italian, or Flemish. There is a Van Eyck . . ."

The dealer and Simon turned, and the dark-haired man who had been outside the doorway was standing not ten feet from them. He had entered so soundlessly that even the Saint had not heard his footsteps on the carpet.

"I am sorry to disturb you," he said to LeGrand in French, "but I must speak with you as soon as possible."

"As you see, I have a customer," LeGrand said with polite deference. "But as soon as . . ."

"This is very urgent," the stranger said, "and I have other duties. If you could spare just a moment . . . alone."

"Very well," LeGrand answered. "If you can excuse me . . ."

He was looking at the Saint, who nodded.

"As a matter of fact," he said, "I may as well be going. I haven't really seen anything that . . ."

LeGrand held up his hand and put on a confidential expression.

"Don't go," he said earnestly. "I have something . . . special. Special for you. Just wait a few moments . . ." He turned to the stranger and motioned him toward an alcove in the rear of the salon, separated from the main area by a pair of velvet curtains. "If you would step this way, please, *Monsieur*. We must be brief."

If the Saint had not been naturally inquisitive, he would have spent many more quiet evenings at home than in fact he did. It would not be accurate to say that he listened to the conversation between Marcel LeGrand and his stolid visitor, but he did not take pains to avoid hearing a phrase here and there from the dialogue of hushed voices.

The first fragment was quite clear, since the newcomer uttered it before he had entered the alcove: "I am Inspector Mathieu . . ." LeGrand's reactions were almost inaudible but had overtones of puzzled incomprehension. Inspector Mathieu mentioned a young woman, paintings, Leonardo da Vinci. LeGrand said, raising his voice, "But it is unbelievable . . ." Inspector Mathieu went on to insist, at length, that it was quite believable, but the details of his statements were lost as the street door of the salon opened and introduced a period of traffic noise from outside. Then, after a few seconds, the expensive cushioned hush of the salon was inviolate again, and the Saint moved around the end of one of the partitions to see a chic and beautiful woman of about thirty standing inside the doorway. Her outfit of brown suit and gloves did justice to a very deserving figure.

"Monsieur Marcel LeGrand?" she asked in French with a foreign accent so slight that it was impossible to identify.

Simon looked at her honey-colored hair and green eyes, and regretfully admitted that he was not Monsieur LeGrand. At that point LeGrand himself, hearing the voices, came alone very quickly out of the alcove and scurried toward the green-eyed lady. Apparently they had never seen one another before, but were otherwise acquainted. LeGrand was looking at the woman in a peculiar way as he nervously went toward her.

"You are . . ." he began in a low voice.

"Yes," she said.

LeGrand was glancing meaningfully back over his shoulder without completely turning his head.

"Come back in ten minutes," he whispered. "We can talk alone then."

She looked at him with the first traces of indignation. Then, over his shoulder she saw the dark-haired Inspector Mathieu step between the curtains of the alcove and look toward her. Realizing that it was to him that LeGrand's nervous glances referred she suddenly changed her expression and spoke in a completely natural voice.

"Well, if you are busy, *Monsieur*, I shall come back later. I am thinking of something for my husband's birthday."

"I am certain we can furnish the perfect gift for him. Would you care to wait?"

LeGrand had regained his usual sangfroid and was speaking at normal volume.

"No, thank you," the woman said. "Until later."

"*Au revoir*, then. Thank you, madame."

Inspector Mathieu waited by the curtains.

"I hope you have not lost a customer because of me," he said.

"The lady was in a hurry," LeGrand replied. "But of course the sooner we can finish this discussion, the sooner I can get on with my business."

Mathieu looked at the Saint, who no longer had any intention of leaving LeGrand's gallery, where so many fascinating bits of side-play took place in the course of an afternoon, until he had satisfied his curiosity as to what was going on. He stood his ground and looked mildly back at Mathieu, who seemed to grow a little uneasy under the gaze of those brilliant blue eyes.

"Well," the Inspector said, "I believe I have given you all the facts . . ."

"Facts!" LeGrand said, rolling his eyes toward the ceiling. "Fantasies would be a better word."

"We shall see," Mathieu said.

He bowed slightly to the art dealer, granted the Saint a slight nod of his head, and walked to the door. LeGrand did not accompany him all the way, and just before stepping out onto the sidewalk the Inspector paused and spoke over his shoulder.

"We have kept this quite secret," he said. "If you wish to speak with me on this subject, call me only at the number I have given you."

When he was gone, Marcel LeGrand exhaled like an underwater swimmer surfacing at the limit of his endurance. His body seemed to sag a little and he put one hand over his heart, which apparently was going a good deal faster than its normal rate.

"I think I've been missing something," the Saint remarked. "I never realized there was quite so much excitement in the art business."

"Nor did I," LeGrand said weakly. "If I survive all this I think I shall retire."

"You asked me to stay," Simon said. "I hope that means you're intending to tell me what 'all this' is about—or did it just mean you still want to sell me something?"

LeGrand sank down on a bright purple leather chair in the center of the display room and motioned Simon to take its yellow mate.

"Both," he answered. "I both wanted to tell you something and at the same time interest you as a buyer. This sudden intrusion of the police was completely unexpected."

The Saint had taken the chair which LeGrand had offered. He settled back and crossed his long legs.

"And Mata Hari?" he asked.

"Pardon?" said LeGrand.

"That lovely creature you shooed out of here a minute ago."

"Ah, she," the dealer said. "Yes, she is a part of what we are calling 'all this.' She is almost the most important part."

"Almost?"

"Yes. What she *has* is the most important."

The Saint smiled reflectively.

"Having seen her, I wouldn't question that . . . except to ask if you have anything specific in mind."

LeGrand leaned forward, his hands clasped between his knees. His voice was low, secretive, and almost melodramatically intense.

"To leave all humor aside, this is truthfully the most fantastic thing which has ever happened to me. It is an art dealer's dream—if it is true—and the greatest art discovery of this century. The young woman you saw here may have in her possession five paintings—three Leonardo da Vincis, one Titian, and one Raphael—which until now were not known to exist, and any one of which would be worth more than all the paintings in this room put together."

2

Marcel LeGrand had no time to continue his explanation. The door of the room opened and the same woman who had come in a few minutes before stepped from the sunlight into the strangely artificial atmosphere of the salon.

"I am sorry, *Monsieur*," she said. "I am afraid I cannot continue to wait. If you . . ."

Marcel LeGrand was instantly on his feet, hurrying toward her and showing every sign of being ready to prostrate himself on the carpet in front of her. With simultaneous shrugs, wags of his head, and wavings of his hands he shepherded her toward the cluster of four chairs in the center of the room, apologizing every step of the way. Simon was standing, waiting with more outward nonchalance than he actually felt. His interest had been aroused, but more than that, he was experiencing that peculiar sense of involvement that had so often marked the point of no return in his adventures—a feeling of fated inclusion in a course of events in whose beginnings he had had no part, but in whose outcome he was destined to play a crucial role. He had no idea how he might become further involved in LeGrand's business, but he suddenly had no doubt that he had had only a taste of what was to come.

"You will understand my behavior when you hear what happened," LeGrand was saying to his new guest. "It was an impossible situation, and there was nothing I could do but ask you to leave."

The woman looked at Simon icily.

"I see that you still have business," she said to LeGrand. "Perhaps I should go elsewhere."

That sent the dealer into renewed paroxysms of apology and entreaty.

"This gentleman is Monsieur Simon Templar, a most valued client and a man completely to be trusted," LeGrand concluded. "You must have heard of him? The Saint?"

The woman's green eyes revealed nothing.

"I lead a rather sheltered life," she said.

"In any case, please be seated," LeGrand implored her. "Monsieur Templar, this is Mademoiselle Lambrini."

She did not offer her gloved hand, but acknowledged the introduction with not much more than a glance as she sat down in the chair which LeGrand offered her.

"I thought I had made it clear," she said, "that our business was to be confidential."

"And so it is!" LeGrand protested.

"With no exceptions," Mademoiselle Lambrini said, looking pointedly at Simon.

"*Mademoiselle,*" LeGrand said, "believe me, he is to be trusted, and will perhaps play a part in our transaction. And let me add very quickly that there are already exceptions—which I knew nothing about. The man who was here when you came the first time was from the police."

Mademoiselle Lambrini finally reacted with something other than frosty calm. Her eyes narrowed and her hands unconsciously moved over one another with nervous agitation in her lap.

"What did they want?" she asked. "The police, I mean. They could have no interest in me."

"But they have," LeGrand said. "The Inspector—Mathieu was his name—instructed me to telephone him if I should be approached by a woman with rare paintings to sell."

"Why?" Mademoiselle Lambrini asked.

She seemed nervous, as Simon had noticed as soon as she heard about the investigator from the police—and yet she seemed genuinely surprised and puzzled that the police should be taking any interest. Simon felt strongly that the probings of the police were a new and unexpected factor in her plans, and a factor which she really could not explain to herself.

"He did not tell me," LeGrand replied. "He said only that if such a person should contact me with paintings to sell I should contact the police because they wished to interview her."

"And you told them . . . what?" she asked.

"Nothing. But I would appreciate an explanation from you."

"I have none," she said. "I can think of no reason why the police, even if they should have heard about my paintings, would have any interest in them. But of course it does seem that all the world is hearing about them very rapidly."

She was looking at the Saint again.

"If there is no reason for the police to be interested in them, why should you be ashamed of letting the world hear about them?" Simon asked.

Mademoiselle Lambrini drew herself up haughtily.

"*Monsieur*, I assure you that I am not ashamed in the slightest. But I am discreet, and for good reason. Monsieur LeGrand has apparently already told you about my paintings. They are not the sort of possessions a woman, living alone, advertises for everybody on earth to hear about. If Monsieur LeGrand is unwilling to respect my wishes about this, there are plenty of other dealers in Paris who would be delighted to hear about them."

"*Mademoiselle*," LeGrand responded with dignity, "if everything is in order, we can conclude this matter tomorrow. Such things cannot be kept secret for long, especially if the police are interested. They will be contacting other dealers all over Paris. But I am willing to tell this Inspector Mathieu nothing if you are willing to trust me and the one or two people I may take into my confidence before I actually pay you for the paintings. Isn't that fair enough?"

"Whom else would you tell—besides Monsieur Templar?" the woman asked.

"The only other I have in mind is an expert on the Italian Renaissance—an old friend of mine I would wish to corroborate my judgment of the paintings. You certainly could not object to that."

"But I understood that you were the greatest expert in France," Mademoiselle Lambrini said.

"In many ways," LeGrand said matter-of-factly. "But in a situation of this sort, with masterpieces of such magnitude, I would not dare to trust my own evaluation alone."

"You've seen the paintings?" Simon asked him.

"I have seen a number of color photographs," LeGrand said. "They include extreme detail. I am already quite satisfied, tentatively, one might say. I have no doubt that Professor . . . my friend will agree as soon as he has seen the canvases themselves."

"And when will this be?" Mademoiselle Lambrini asked.

"Tomorrow morning?" LeGrand suggested. "Would you prefer to have the paintings brought here?"

"I would prefer that you come to my house. Just a moment."

She took a pen and small leather-bound pad from her purse and wrote out an address.

"I trust you can find this," she said, giving the piece of paper to LeGrand. "It's a white house, set back from the road, surrounded with high hedges."

They discussed directions for finding the house while the Saint watched in silence, wondering just how he could insure that his acquaintance with Mademoiselle Lambrini could be kept active and developing. He would have had the same thoughts even if there had not been paintings and police and a couple of million dollars involved . . . some of which might eventually be coaxed into his own pockets. Miss Lambrini was what in the coarser forms of detective fiction might have been called a doll. She had the sort of imperious beauty that seems challenging the world to conquer it, and the continuing sight of her had the same effect on Simon that the sight of Mount Everest must have on a dedicated mountain climber.

She got to her feet with the same crisp abruptness that had characterised all her movements.

"Very well," she said. "Ten-thirty in the morning. I should have preferred today because I have my own plans to consider, but if you can come to a decision tomorrow I shall be satisfied."

"I trust we shall all be satisfied," LeGrand said. "And I shall have my check book with me."

"Good. I hope I can trust both of you to refrain from discussing this with anyone. I have . . . specific reasons to worry."

A shadow crossed her face when she spoke the last words. Simon took it as a cue.

"Maybe you should tell us more about that side of things," he said.

"I need no help," she replied. "Good day."

They were at the door, and LeGrand opened it for her.

"Good day, Mademoiselle Lambrini. Monsieur Templar, if you will remain here briefly I can show you . . ."

"I think I'll walk with Mademoiselle Lambrini," the Saint told him. "You'll hear from me later today."

"I have told you I need no help," the woman said. "I'm quite capable of walking unassisted."

"I won't offer you my protection, then," the Saint said amiably. "Just my charming company."

"I had hoped that you might be interested in Mademoiselle Lambrini's paintings," LeGrand said. "It is certainly the opportunity of a lifetime to share in."

"At the moment I'm more interested in Mademoiselle Lambrini," Simon said hurriedly. "I'll telephone you. She's getting away."

She was in fact out of the door and walking quickly out of viewing range from the windows of the salon. The Saint ignored LeGrand's protestations, shook the dealer's nervously damp hand, and strode away after the woman. He could see her blonde head among the people gathered at a crossing half a block away. She turned to the left at the intersection, but the Saint was already gaining on her rapidly. She was easy to follow, taller than most women, and the afternoon sun made a beacon of the lightness of her hair.

About five doors down the new street she had taken, the Saint caught up with her. Before she noticed him he quietly fell into step alongside her. When she happened to look round and notice him she gave a start and then a short humorless laugh.

"Is there more than one of you?" she asked, still in that tantalizingly accented French. "Or are you the same gentleman I asked to leave me alone just a minute ago?"

As she spoke her sharp heels continued their staccato on the pavement. Simon needed only his most casual walking speed to keep abreast of her.

"I won't try to match your subtle wit," he answered with the faintest trace of sarcasm. "I'll just ask if you would care to join me for a drink."

She stopped beneath the awning of a jewelry shop.

"Monsieur Templar, I am not certain just what your connection with Monsieur LeGrand and his interest in my paintings is. Perhaps you are a rich American who is going to put up the money for all five, or perhaps you are a spy of his hoping to find out something which will give him an advantage in our bargaining. In either case, or whatever the case may be, I do not stand to benefit from your company."

She moved on, and Simon continued unruffled beside her.

"Maybe I'm just lonely," he said. "Don't you have a soft spot in your heart for visiting art lovers?"

"There are girls in bars for that sort of thing," she said drily. "I'll leave you now. There is my automobile."

They were at the entrance of a narrow one-way street. Illegally parked there was a single black Mercedes facing away from the Saint and Mademoiselle Lambrini. Through the rear window Simon could make out the peaked cap of a chauffeur.

"Well," he said to her, "at least we have something in common: neither of us finds the other one very pleasant."

For a moment he thought she was going to smile, but then she nodded, said *"Bonjour,"* and walked away toward the Mercedes.

"Au revoir," the Saint said.

He watched her until she had reached the car, and then he started back toward LeGrand's salon. He had scarcely taken the first step when he heard a short sharp scream. It was almost lost in the traffic noise, and the passersby near him did not seem even to notice it. He spun around in time to see Mademoiselle Lambrini being pulled into the black Mercedes. The automobile's door was half open, and the woman's struggles had succeeded in keeping one of her arms and one of her legs outside the car.

Simon ran toward the car. The only other witness to the scene was an old woman, her arms full of parcels, standing and gaping as dumbly as if she had been watching the whole thing on television.

The Saint reached the black car just before Mademoiselle Lambrini could be hauled inside clear of the door. He threw himself between the open door and the side of the car, so that the door could not be closed. There were two men immediately visible—one the man in the chauffeur's cap and the other the man trying to restrain Mademoiselle Lambrini. The latter had to give up the hold of one of his hands on the woman in order to aim a punch at the Saint's midriff. Simon evaded the jab, caught the man's forearm, and yanked him by his outstretched arm straight out of the door, banging the kidnapper's head and shoulder against the doorframe in the process.

Mademoiselle Lambrini swung her purse at the head of the driver as he started to throw the Mercedes into gear. The automobile lurched forward with the door still open, the Saint clinging to the outside, and its comely owner bashing its driver with a large alligator purse.

It was a short trip—not more than half a dozen yards. The driver slammed on the brake, flung open his own door, and jumped out before the car had stopped moving. In the meanwhile, his comrade had scrambled to his feet and was disappearing past the gaping old woman with the parcels. The Saint might have caught the escaping driver if the Mercedes, in coming to an abrupt halt as its wheels bumped into the curb, had not given such a jerk that he was thrown momentarily off balance. He half fell, and saw that Mademoiselle Lambrini had been thrown forward against the dashboard. Clutching her head with one hand, she slumped half out of the still rumbling car, and the Saint had to catch her in his arms and raise her back to a sitting position in the front seat. By the time he could look up both of the men were out of sight.

Simon gently took Mademoiselle Lambrini's hand and moved it away from her forehead.

"Cut?" he asked.

"No," she said weakly. "I am all right."

"I thought so," he continued with confident good cheer. "Somebody was telling me just a few minutes ago that you are the sort of girl who doesn't need protection, and now it's perfectly obvious that that's true." He straightened up and nodded. "I'll be running along then, and . . ."

She let out a dismayed gasp and caught his arm.

"No! Please. Don't leave me. I . . . I thought you were one of them."

"One of them?"

"I'll explain if you won't leave me . . ."

From his standing position the Saint saw something on the floor behind the front seat of the Mercedes. He also noticed the old woman of the parcels creeping tentatively nearer, one hesitant step at a time, as several other pedestrians gathered at the end of the narrow street to look at and discuss the situation.

"I won't leave you, then—yet," Simon said. "But we'd better leave here. For one thing, there seems to be a body in the back seat of your car."

3

"A body?"

Mademoiselle Lambrini turned to peer over into the back of the Mercedes as Simon opened the rear door. A middle-aged man in a black suit lay unconscious on the floor, face up, his arms sprawled awkwardly as they had fallen when he was dumped there.

"Hans!" she cried, in shocked recognition.

"One of ours?" Simon asked.

"My chauffeur," she answered in a voice that was genuinely shaken with concern. "Have they hurt him? What . . ."

The Saint could see that the man was breathing deeply. There was a faint smell of chloroform on the air.

"I think they just doped him. Let's see how his pulse is doing."

When he had lifted the man up onto the back seat, he realized that the audience of pedestrians which had started to collect at a distance a few moments before was gathering closer around the car. At any minute some alert member of the Parisian police would stumble on the scene and begin asking questions.

"Let's either sell tickets or pull out of here," Simon said. "If you'd like to drive I'll tend to your friend here."

"I can't," Mademoiselle Lambrini said. Then she noticed that the half dozen people around the car were cocking their ears to listen. Her next words were in excellently pronounced English. "I can't drive. Will you, please? If I could trouble you . . ."

"Of course," the Saint said, also in English. "Would you like to get back here with Otto?"

She was already sliding onto the seat next to the limp man. He was about sixty-five with close-cropped gray hair.

"Hans is his name," she said. "Please, let's hurry."

The Saint nodded pleasantly to the little group of gawkers, got into the driver's seat, and started the automobile's engine.

"Where to?" he asked over his shoulder.

"Would you mind . . . would it be too much trouble to ask you to drive me home?"

"I don't know whether it's too much trouble for you to ask me or not, but it won't be too much trouble for me to do it."

She flushed.

"You are making a joke about my English."

Simon backed the car a few inches from the curb, shifted it into forward gear, and felt the powerful engine move it smoothly away from the group of onlookers.

"I shouldn't have made a joke," he said. "You speak very good English . . . and I'd guess about ten other languages, judging from the fact that I can't place your accent."

He was turning the Mercedes into a main street. She met his eyes in the rear-view mirror for an instant and then suddenly bent over her chauffeur.

"Here we are chattering away as if we were at a tea party, with poor Hans lying here in such a terrible condition," she said. "What can I do for him?"

"His breathing seems strong enough. Let him sleep it off. Or when you get home you can phone a doctor." The Saint turned his head so as to see her again in the rear-view mirror. "Speaking of home, where is it?"

"I'm afraid it's fifty kilometers out of Paris."

Simon sighed.

"I asked for it. Fifty kilometers in any particular direction?"

She told him the way.

"Are you sure you don't mind?" she concluded.

"No . . . assuming that a girl with a house full of Leonardos has an equally good kitchen and wine cellar, or at least a decent bottle of scotch."

She smiled.

"If your standards aren't too terribly high I might be able to satisfy you."

The Saint returned her smile.

"I'd be willing to bet on it. And for a start, you might try satisfying my curiosity about these bully boys who wanted to borrow you along with your car."

Her green eyes, reflected in the mirror, were wide with surprise at his question.

"How would I know that?" she asked. "I didn't invite them for a ride, I can tell you that."

Simon navigated a difficult forking in the river of traffic, kept on his course south out of the city, and then turned his attention back to his one conscious passenger, who in the interim had been trying to revive the unconscious one.

"And I suppose you have no idea why they decided to kidnap you," he said.

"Of course. They undoubtedly wanted my paintings. That's what you're thinking, isn't it?"

"I'm trying to keep an open mind," he answered. "Maybe they were going to hold you for ransom. If these paintings have been kept as secret as you and LeGrand seem to think, it's possible that what just happened wasn't even connected with them . . . but you'd know what the chances of that are much better than I would."

There was a bitter tone in her laugh.

"Who would pay any ransom for me?"

"Your father? Brother?"

"I have no family any more," she told him curtly. "The paintings—and poor Hans here—are all I have in any way tied to the past."

"Could they have expected you to pay your own way out?" Simon asked.

"No more than they might have expected anybody else in Paris to make it worth their trouble. I am not rich. I own this car and my clothes and such things . . ."

"Such as a few paintings worth several million dollars," the Saint put in.

"But I have only a monthly income I inherited," she continued. "Not enough to make anyone think of kidnapping me."

"Then it must be the paintings they were after," Simon said. "Paintings nobody is supposed to know about. Which is an interesting fact in itself. How is it that five such fantastically rare paintings have been lying around your house all this time without being heard of?"

"It's even more interesting when you know the full story," she replied. "I will tell you later. Now I think that Hans is waking up."

The Saint caught glimpses of the revival of Mademoiselle Lambrini's chauffeur. Most of his attention had to be focused on keeping Mademoiselle Lambrini's Mercedes from destruction at the hands of homeward bound suburban drivers. But before the worst of the evening rush hour had swamped the roads of the city's outskirts he had managed to get well along the N7 to the south, past the vicinity of Orly airfield and on the way to Fontainebleau.

"We turn soon," Mademoiselle Lambrini said to him presently. "Follow the signs toward Barbizon."

Hans was sitting up beside her now, still apparently too dazed to be sure of anything except the fact that his professional duties had been taken over by somebody else.

"I drive," he said feebly.

"Bleiben Sie ruhig," the woman told him. "Relax. You aren't even awake yet. That is Mr Templar driving. Mr Templar, this is Hans Kraus. He has been with my family since I was a girl."

"How do you do, Hans?" said the Saint cheerily. "Feeling better after your nap?"

Suddenly the chauffeur seemed to come entirely awake, as if for the first time he fully realized where he was and what had happened.

"A man!" he said excitedly. "He asked me for a match, und den ven I turned—I vas in der car—he pushed somet'ing over my face. I could not even shout, und everyt'ing vas coming very dark . . . I don't know, then . . ."

"They used chloroform, or something like it," Simon said.

"But vy? Vat happened?"

"There were two of them," his mistress explained. "One wore your hat, and then when I walked up to the car they pulled me inside. If Mr Templar hadn't come along . . . I don't know."

"Did you get a good look at the man?" Simon asked, tossing the words over his shoulder. "Was he French?"

Hans Kraus shook his head, rubbing his cheek with one hand.

"I don't know. He did not speak to me. He looked . . . nothing special. But I think I vould know him."

Mademoiselle Lambrini interrupted suddenly.

"Oh! You turn there . . . just ahead. To the left. And then go slowly. We are almost to the house."

The Mercedes had been traveling through an area where the land seemed cultivated more for beauty than for agricultural production, and the countryside, mostly wooded, was divided into small estates, each with its house scarcely visible through tailored shrubs and trees.

Simon reduced speed.

"Nice neighborhood," he said. "Have you lived here very long?"

"No." She leaned forward and pointed past his shoulder. "Turn in there, where you see the stone wall."

The Saint guided the car into the drive, which formed a U-shaped loop from the road to the two-storeyed brick house that dominated the acre of property from a shallow rise. The grounds were thickly shaded with trees. Between the house and the road, on sloping leaf-covered terrain, was an inoperative fountain watched over by a nude marble nymph, her hands carefully arranged in the sort of modest pose affected by marble nymphs when they watch over the fountains of the respectable well-to-do.

Simon stopped the black Mercedes at the front door of the house and helped his two passengers out onto the gravel drive. Hans Kraus was unsteady on his feet, but when Mademoiselle Lambrini tried to help support him he pulled himself up with a great effort at dignity and made his way with little assistance up the steps. He held the door open after his mistress unlocked it, and then swayed dizzily.

Simon caught his arm.

"All right?"

The man took a deep breath.

"*Ja*. Better. Thank you."

"Off to bed with you," Mademoiselle Lambrini said to him.

Kraus looked back through the trees in front of the house as the Saint closed the door.

"But *Fräulein*, they may have found out about this place. They may come here!"

"A lot you could do about it in your condition," she said gently. "Go to your bed, *mon vieux*. You have taken care of me often enough. Let me take care of you."

The white-haired man shrugged.

"As you vill, *Fräulein*. But be careful, please." He gave Simon a distrustful look, bowed slightly, and moved slowly away down the entrance hall toward the door at its far end. He turned to speak once more. "Excuse me please."

"Take care of yourself," said the Saint casually.

"And I shall bring you some supper," Mademoiselle Lambrini said.

She led the Saint out of the dim hall into the house's large front living room. A large window looked south over the entrance drive, the marble nymph, and her dry fountain. The room itself was not as richly furnished as Simon had expected. What was there fitted harmoniously, was antique, and gave the impression of having been there for a long time—and of having cost someone plenty a good many years before. It was just that there was so little of it: a sofa, three chairs, a pair of small tables, an empty glass-fronted mahogany cabinet. Yet the room was very large, and the empty spaces where furniture had formerly stood were depressingly evident. The walls, too, were bare except for two etchings of hunting scenes.

The owner of the house sensed the meaning of Simon's survey.

"I am selling this place," she said. "I have already sold quite a few things from it, as you can see."

"It does seem large for a single girl."

"Yes," she said very thoughtfully, as if considering whether or not to say something further. The decision was positive. "If I can truly be called single."

Simon frowned slightly.

"You're married or have been?"

"I am married, Monsieur Templar—to these."

She was walking to a recessed bookcase of about her own height, next to the marble fireplace. Her fingers touched something on the left side of the bookcase, and then she easily slid the entire bookcase, shelves, and back panel aside into the wall. Behind it was a space like a wide shallow closet, containing something that resembled an irregularly shaped waist-high box covered with a green cloth.

Mademoiselle Lambrini pulled away the cloth, revealing the five paintings which stood there in a crude rack, or at least their frames, since only the front canvas was visible. At a glance the Saint recognized the style of Leonardo da Vinci. Even in the sunset light the colors had the luster of emeralds and rubies. It was the half-length portrait of a woman against a background of lakes and mountains.

One by one Mademoiselle Lambrini showed Simon the pictures and unnecessarily told him the names of the artists. Then she put the cloth back over them and slid the bookcase into place again in front of the secret compartment.

"They're beautiful," Simon said, "and I'm sure very valuable."

"Very. They are worth at least eight million francs—a million and a half dollars."

"And they're yours," Simon said, allowing a distinct note of doubt to come into his voice.

"Of course—until I sell them tomorrow."

"Just a few lucky finds you picked up for a song at some little place on the Left Bank?"

She turned and glared at him coldly from near the marble fireplace.

"If you are going to make stupid remarks about them I shall be sorry I showed them to you. You gave me good reason to think I could trust you, Monsieur Templar, and . . ."

"Since we're getting intimate enough to have quarrels, won't you call me Simon? And I'll call you . . ."

He stopped, questioningly.

"Annabella," she said without relaxing.

"Anna the beautiful," Simon translated. "Very appropriate . . . very true."

She blushed slightly and tried to keep her lips from softening into the hint of a smile.

"You don't need to flatter me, Monsieur Templar. You have already saved my life—and my paintings. That is enough for one day."

"I'm just giving my natural honesty free rein," the Saint said engagingly. "And you can't blame me for feeling some curiosity, too. I didn't mean to insult you or your one-woman Louvre."

She nodded, and this time she actually did smile, although a little tiredly.

"I apologize, too. I am very nervous. This sale to Marcel LeGrand means everything to me—and I'm not accustomed to being kidnapped either, or almost kidnapped. The strain of trying to arrange this deal with LeGrand was enough before I found out today that someone else knows about these paintings and wants to steal them."

"Do you know that for certain?" the Saint asked her.

"After what happened in Paris, it's a reasonable assumption, isn't it?" she replied. "I assure you I don't know of any other reason why anybody should bother me. I have very little money and no rich relatives."

"Maybe what seems very little money to you might seem a lot to other people," Simon suggested.

She shook her head.

"No. I literally have just enough money to keep up appearances—though why I'm telling you all this I don't know."

She hesitated. Simon, lounging against the wall near the front window, looked at her across the darkening room.

"I must be a sort of rejuvenated Father Figure," he surmised. "People always confess to me. Can't help themselves. Luckily I'm entirely trustworthy except where money and women are concerned—so if you don't have a bank account or a husband, both of us are safe."

She laughed uncertainly.

"Well, I have neither. My father died just a few months ago, and he left me this house. It was heavily mortgaged, and almost all the proceeds from it will have to go to settle debts. In fact I have had to sell furniture in order to live these past weeks. I didn't have the heart to sell the car. Hans is so fond of it, and he stays with me for nothing. He lives on his own savings." She brightened. "Of course I've also known I would only have to hold out for a few more weeks, and then I would be rich—from selling the paintings."

"Which brings us back to . . ."

But Simon did not have a chance to finish. Hans Kraus came running from the back rooms of the house, shouting at the top of his voice.

4

"*Fräulein! Fräulein! Bitte schnell!* Quickly!"

The Saint and Annabella Lambrini met the gray-haired chauffeur in the entrance hall.

"Hans!" she cried. "What is it?"

"A man! I haf seen a man from my vindow. T'rough der trees he valked! Und ven I go out after him, he ran to der front."

Simon did not wait to hear any more of the story. He was already on his way out the front door of the house after only an instant's glance to make certain he was not walking into an ambush. At first the most nearly human thing he saw in the golden twilight was the modest marble nymph. Then his keen eye caught a flash of color in motion far down among the trees near the main road. Although it was already obvious that he had little chance of catching up with the intruder, he went through the motions of chasing him just in case some miracle should occur that would make the effort worthwhile.

But when he reached the dry fountain and paused, the Saint heard the engine of a car roaring from first into second gear with a squeal of rubber on pavement. He could not see the car that was making the noise, but its sound told him that it was taking off in the general direction of Paris as fast as it could go.

Simon felt vaguely unhappy with himself. If the Mercedes had been followed while he was driving it, he should have noticed. He had in fact kept his eyes open for anybody tailing him on the way out from the city and had seen nothing that aroused his suspicions. But the roads had been crowded, and if the followers had held well back while Annabella Lambrini's car was in the main traffic stream they would have been hard to spot. On the other hand, they might not have followed at all. Knowing as much as they appeared to, they would presumably have found out where she lived.

"Did you see anything?" she was calling to him.

He turned and strode back up the slope, where he was met by Annabella Lambrini and her chauffeur on the driveway.

"Just an art connoisseur dropping in to have a look at your collection," he answered. "He's shy, though. I never got near him." He looked back down toward the road. "Too bad. I might have caught a ride back to Paris."

The woman's lovely green eyes were much wider when Simon turned back to meet them than they had been a few seconds before.

"You are not leaving!" she exclaimed.

"I didn't know I was invited to stay," he said, with the most feather-light touch of challenge.

"Oh, please do! Don't leave us here alone tonight—the last night before I finally get these paintings off my hands. Hans isn't feeling well, and I . . ."

"I feel good," Hans said. "I am not longer ill."

"I don't think Hans trusts me," murmured the Saint.

Annabella Lambrini smiled indulgently. They were moving slowly back up the front steps of the house.

"Hans is just overprotective. He's a worrier, aren't you, Hans?"

"I don't know why," Simon said. "Working for a girl with such a nice uncomplicated life as yours."

Hans turned to the Saint as they entered the hall.

"It is no personal, ah, feeling against you, Sir," he said stiffly. "The lady iss not safe, und only I am here to protect her. No father, no family. Und I am not young und not strong. Ve must be foresighted . . . dot is . . ."

"Careful?" Simon offered.

"*Ja*, careful. You understand?"

"I understand. In fact, I think your attitude is more sensible than the lady's." He watched her wryly as he was speaking. "Here I am, one of the most notorious pirates on the face of the earth, and she's offering to take me under her roof for her own protection."

She looked him in the eye.

"I trust you are an honorable man . . . Simon."

The way she pronounced his first name, for the first time, would have been enough to send warm tremors up and down the spinal ganglia of a less controlled man. As it was, the Saint held himself detached from the more obvious effects of that sensuous voice and merely decided that becoming Miss Lambrini's personal cavalier might have more rewards than he had anticipated.

"If you trust that I'm honorable, you're very trusting," he remarked.

"I have reason to trust you . . . and without you I seem quite certain to lose not only my paintings but possibly my life."

They were in the living room now, and Hans Kraus turned on the lights. The sun was already below the horizon, and the molten glow of the sky was cooling to darkness. Annabella Lambrini drew the curtains over the large window.

"Have you any idea who these characters might be?" Simon asked her. "The ones who are so anxious to get their hands on you and your property?"

"No. Not the slightest."

"Or how they might have found out about the paintings?"

"No." She looked at Kraus, who was standing near the door as if waiting for orders. "Go rest now. Monsieur Templar will be staying—won't you, Simon?"

"My fate seems to be sealed," he said resignedly. "I will be staying."

"Good," the chauffeur said. "I make it certain that all is locked."

"Are there any outside lights?" the Saint asked. "If there are, I suggest you leave them on all night. With a million and a half dollars you can afford to run up an electric bill."

The chauffeur bowed briefly and went out.

"I am grateful, Simon," Annabella said warmly. "I realize that it is not very . . . conventional to ask this of you, but the fact is, I am not a very conventional female. I have led my life as it pleased me, not wanting to be tied—at least not until I had enjoyed myself. And I knew, from my father, that I would have money coming, though I was not sure until after he died just where it was expected to come from. But I have always been independent, perhaps partly because of the idea that I would have a great deal of money some day. My relationships with men have not had to be on the careful practical basis that most women worry about. In a word, I haven't learned to give a damn what people think of me. You are shocked?"

"I'm favorably impressed," Simon said. "It doesn't sound like a typically Italian attitude."

"I am not typically Italian." She waved him toward a chair. "Sit down, please. My father was from the Italian Tyrol, and my mother was from Munich. I was sent to Sweden when I was a little child, during the war. My mother was killed in an air raid in Munich. My father was in the Italian army on the Russian front. He disappeared completely, like so many others, as the Russians moved on Europe, but he survived as a prisoner until he was released and found me years later. I was fifteen years old by then . . . and yet I still remembered him."

The Saint nodded as she paused.

"And then you came to live in France?" he said. "You've led quite a cosmopolitan life."

"I've never really lived here for long," she said. "I suffer from *Wanderlust*, you might say. In fact I have every intention of taking my money when I've sold these paintings and going to California and building myself a gorgeous house and living like a movie star . . . and marrying for love."

"Like a movie star?" said the Saint cynically.

She smiled and went to the door.

"Would you care for some sherry before dinner? It's all we have. The supply of alcohol is rather limited. It's a strange feeling, living on nothing but appearances one day and expecting millions the next."

Simon said he would like the sherry. When his hostess came back with it, after a delay caused by starting a leg of lamb roasting in the oven, she found him inspecting the sliding bookcase—which was not sliding, but still in place.

"Clever," he said. "I assume you press one of the shelves to open it?"

Annabella handed him a bottle of Dry Sack, and put down the two glasses she carried.

"You are interested in carpentry?" she asked, arching an eyebrow.

"Was it one of your father's hobbies?" the Saint countered, uncorking the bottle and pouring for both of them.

He left the shelves and sat down near the woman on the sofa. She looked beautiful and he liked her—and for those reasons among others he had no intention of swiping her paintings and keeping all the loot for himself, although of course he did anticipate a reasonable material reward for the troubles he had already gone through as well as those he probably still had in store.

"I don't know who built it," she said. "I know very little about my father, really."

"And the paintings?"

"Even less. My father was from an aristocratic family. Before the war they were rich and owned property in many countries. This house, for example, had been in the family for several generations. During the war, things fell apart. These paintings, as I understand it, had been in the family for a long time. To my father, they were not an investment—a way of making money. They were a trust. He made certain they were hidden before he went to fight the Communists. Then he told me as he saw the war was going to be lost, he was afraid that the Communists very possibly would take over Austria and Italy, and of course would confiscate private property. He sent instructions for the paintings to be taken out through the Alps to Switzerland by his sister. Then, as I told you, he was captured by the Russians and held for years. When he came back, his sister was dead. He didn't tell me the details, but somehow he located the paintings. He did not want to sell them, but when he died this year he told me they were all he had to leave me, that I would find them here in this house, and that I should sell them with no publicity to a reputable dealer."

The Saint sipped his sherry meditatively. Annabella Lambrini seemed genuinely moved as she told the end of her story. She had lowered her eyes, and now she sat without speaking.

"Don't feel you're smashing up the family tradition," he said. "Three Leonardos and a Titian or two thrown in are quite a bit for any woman to live with. I think LeGrand is your best bet, unless you can afford a mansion and a small private army."

She raised her eyes and looked at him with a new expression.

"I think you are the only army I need, or want," she said.

"And I've never had a pleasanter job of guard duty," the Saint replied.

He raised his glass, and she raised hers, and the crystal bubbles touched with the sound of tiny bells, and Simon wondered if he believed a single word of what she had told him.

5

There were no disturbances that night. Whoever was after Annabella Lambrini's little cache of masterpieces had apparently given up trying to take them by storm, at least for the time being. By nine-thirty in the morning the Lambrini household was a picture of commonplace and cozy normality. A completely recovered Hans Kraus was out in the gravel driveway washing the Mercedes with hose and chamois, and Simon and Annabella were polishing off the last of eggs, rolls, jam, and coffee in the bright dining room. The Saint looked out through the large window at the chauffeur moving around the streaming black car and released a contented sigh.

"I must have been born with royal blood in my veins," he said. "There's nothing that gives me a greater sense of well-being than sitting at a late breakfast with a beautiful woman and watching other people work."

Annabella smiled. She was not only visibly excited about the fortune the day was supposed to bring her, she seemed absolutely radiant compared with the tense tired state she had been in the evening before.

"After this morning I won't let Hans work," she said happily. "He deserves to retire."

"Are you sure he wants to? Some people thrive on hard labor."

"I can't imagine it."

The Saint chuckled.

"Neither can I. It makes me think of a prison sentence." He looked at his watch. "When is it you're going to legally raid the banks of France?"

"LeGrand said he would be here with his friend at ten-thirty. Maybe we should put the paintings out for him to see."

"They are still there, aren't they?"

She laughed.

"I've checked three times already. They're quite safe."

Before Simon heard or saw a car approaching the house he noticed through the window that Hans Kraus had paused in his polishing and was peering down the driveway toward the road.

"I think he's here," he said, getting up from the table. "Or somebody."

Annabella was fidgeting like a schoolgirl before her first dance.

"Don't tease me. Or somebody, indeed! It will be him. It has to be him!"

It was LeGrand. The Saint recognized his dark-bearded head as a frog-nosed blue Citroën crunched to a halt near the Mercedes. There was no one else with him in the car. Annabella Lambrini almost ran for the front door. Outside, Hans Kraus, looking fiercely protective, had taken up a position by the front steps as if preparing to repel boarders.

Still making his way at a fairly leisurely rate toward the entrance hall, Simon heard Annabella exclaiming in French as she opened the door to LeGrand.

"Oh, I am so glad to see you, *Monsieur*! Come in, please. Did you have trouble finding my house?"

"Blind intuition would have led me here, I am sure," LeGrand said elegantly. "What a great day this is for both of us, *n'est-ce pas?*"

"*Vraiment, Monsieur, vraiment!*"

Simon joined the enthusiastic pair in the hallway, greeted LeGrand and shook hands with him.

"What a surprise!" LeGrand blurted. Then he covered his surprise smoothly. "I had no idea that you two charming people would have become friends . . . so . . ."

"So early in the morning?" Annabella said archly.

Marcel LeGrand only shrugged and smiled.

"If it were not for Monsieur Templar I would probably not be here this morning to meet you," Annabella told him. "And neither would my paintings."

LeGrand looked shocked, and the woman gave him a detailed account of what had happened after she had left his gallery the afternoon before.

"These men: you have seen nothing more of them since yesterday evening?" LeGrand asked nervously.

"No," she answered, darting a fond look at the Saint. "I think that when they discovered I was not alone here with my chauffeur—who is no longer strong enough at his age to be much protection—they gave up their ideas of robbing me."

LeGrand was stroking his beard thoughtfully. "Assuming their object was robbery," he said.

The three of them were standing in the big front living room now, and Annabella offered them chairs. LeGrand sat down along with the Saint and his hostess and then bobbed up again and began to pace the floor after her next question.

"What other object could they have?" she asked.

"I can think only of the police," LeGrand answered. "This Inspector Mathieu who called on me so inopportunely yesterday. Perhaps he and his fellow bureaucratic bloodhounds are going to desperate lengths to pry into your business. Such things have been known to happen—unofficially."

"Even if that were believable," Annabella said, "why?"

LeGrand turned from his pacing and faced her, his stubby legs apart. It was a way of standing which suggested that he needed to assure a firm support for a torso that clearly showed the cumulative result of several decades of rich cooking.

"Do we need to be surprised at anything a government does?" he asked with sudden passion. "Is there any privacy left anywhere today? When we move from our beds they take an interest!"

The Saint had relaxed totally in his softly upholstered chair. He brought the long fingers of both his hands together against his lips as LeGrand spoke, and then lowered them.

"But still," he intervened politely, "wouldn't these be rather peculiar cops? Your deal with Mademoiselle Lambrini has to be legal. A man of your reputation can't afford under-the-counter games. You pay your taxes, I'm sure—or *enough* of them, at least. And Mademoiselle Lambrini tells me that the paintings have been in her family's hands—legally—for many years. That hardly seems to call for special investigations."

"Maybe they do not have your trusting nature," Annabella said.

LeGrand, still standing at the center of the room, suddenly clapped his hands together and rubbed them briskly.

"What use is it to speculate about this?" he said. "We have more important things to do."

"Certainly, *Monsieur*," Annabella replied eagerly. "It is time for the unveiling."

She got to her feet and went to the bookshelf beside the fireplace.

"Clever," LeGrand said with a giggle of pure nervous anticipation when she pressed the release mechanism and opened the secret compartment in the wall.

Then he froze, his eyes glittering, biting his furry underlip as he waited for Simon and Annabella to uncover the paintings. They removed the cloth covering and stepped back to show the first Leonardo da Vinci.

The art dealer's first audible reaction was a prolonged, awed, "Ahhh . . ." He hurried forward and fell down on his knees in front of the painting, gazing at it with hungrily darting eyes from two or three feet away.

"Oh, exquisite. Magnificent. It is not only real, real Leonardo, but good Leonardo. *Great* Leonardo."

He heaved himself back onto his feet and looked at Annabella, who was smiling joyously.

"You are rich, *Mademoiselle*. This alone will bring . . . well, I don't know how much!"

It amused Simon to see how quickly a cloud of practicality veiled the sun of LeGrand's spontaneous enthusiasm.

"Of course," the dealer said, "things never bring what they are worth. And then there is the interest I must pay on loans, and the problem of . . ."

"Later, *Monsieur*, later," Annabella interrupted good-naturedly. "We can bargain later . . . if you are interested. Would you like to see the others?"

"Would I like to see the others!" LeGrand burbled. "That is the same as asking me if I would like to be twenty-five again! Show me, please. Show me."

His next word was *"Incroyable!"* as with Annabella he brought the second masterpiece from its one-time hiding place into the clear morning light of the room. The ritual and the exclamations and ecstatic comments were repeated until all five of the paintings had been admired.

"This takes my breath away," LeGrand said. "What can I say?"

"Say—ten million francs?" Annabella suggested.

LeGrand looked at her stoically.

"We may bargain, *Mademoiselle*, but I do not think we shall quarrel."

"Well, shall I leave you to haggle?" Simon asked. "I'll take a stroll in the garden."

"Whatever you please, *M'sieur*," LeGrand said.

"Stay if you like," Annabella said simultaneously.

Their responses to his question were entirely automatic. Their consciousnesses were almost exclusively focused on the paintings and the deal to be made, and the Saint felt about as much a part of things as the bride's brother along on a honeymoon. When he left the room they were already so absorbed in financial discussion that they did not even notice his departure.

He went out the front door of the house and sauntered across the drive to the Mercedes, where Kraus was engrossed in putting a final burnish on the mirror-like black shell.

"*Wie geht's, Hans?*" he enquired sociably.

"*Ganz gut, danke, mein Herr.* And you?"

The chauffeur straightened his shoulders as he turned to answer. He wiped his moist forehead with the back of the hand which held the polishing cloth.

"Very well too," Simon said.

"And there?" Hans Kraus asked in a quieter voice, with a tilt of his head toward the house.

He seemed to have become much friendlier to the Saint now that both the paintings and their owner had come through the night unscathed.

"They're talking price."

"He won't cheat her?"

"Hans, you're an incorrigibly suspicious man I'm afraid. LeGrand will drive a hard bargain, but he's honest."

The chauffeur's face became ashamedly apologetic.

"You understand . . . how could I know these things?" he said. "She is only a young woman, with a great responsibility, and I cannot be of much help. I worry. I cannot help it."

"Well, you won't have to worry much longer," Simon told him. "Once LeGrand has the paintings and your *Fräulein* has her money, the Lambrini household can relax indefinitely."

"Will she have it soon?" Kraus asked. "It is all she has thought about for months. There has been almost no sleeping."

"I think she'll have it soon," Simon assured him. "LeGrand was very impressed."

"Let us fervently hope so," Kraus said.

Simon left him and started to stroll across the lawn, wondering just how long the other parties who had been showing such an interest in Annabella's art hoard were going to remain inactive. Then Annabella's own voice called his name and he turned back to the house. She and LeGrand were standing at the front door.

"All finished?" the Saint asked as he rejoined them on the steps.

"We have agreed," the art dealer said. "There is only for my colleague to see the paintings also. He is the only expert in France whose opinion I respect above my own. While I, of course, trust Mademoiselle Lambrini completely, the money involved in this transaction is not all mine, and it is necessary to have a confirmation of my judgment."

Simon glanced at Annabella. She seemed untroubled by any misgivings, and apparently the price they had agreed on pleased her.

"Congratulations to both of you, then," he said. "You won't be needing me any more. Maybe Monsieur LeGrand would be kind enough to give me a ride back into Paris."

"Oh, but I do need you!" Annabella exclaimed.

She took his arm as they followed LeGrand to his car.

"Monsieur LeGrand's friend just called to say he has had car trouble on the road coming out here," she said. "I need you for protection until he comes . . . and then of course I shall need you for the celebration."

The Saint inclined his head gracefully.

"Where celebrations are concerned, my availability is unlimited."

"As you like, *Monsieur*," LeGrand said. "You are welcome to ride with me."

"Monsieur Templar will stay with me," Annabella insisted. "You will be coming back to my house with the professor in any case, won't you?"

LeGrand looked at his wrist watch and shook his head.

"Perhaps not. My wife does not care for managing my business very long. I had to leave her in charge while I drove out here. But I shall see that Professor Clarneau comes to see you as quickly as possible."

"I must admit that I'm impatient," Annabella said.

They walked to LeGrand's car. He paused to shake hands before getting into the driver's seat.

"It was a pleasure, *Mademoiselle*," he said to Annabella. "And an honor, *Monsieur*."

"It will be an even greater pleasure for me when our deal is completed," Annabella said. "What about delivering the paintings . . . and the money?"

LeGrand laughed as he settled himself and closed the car door. He looked up with his elbow on the open window frame.

"I don't blame you for being anxious, *Mademoiselle*. My wife is already as anxious for *me* to sell the paintings so that she can have a certain fur coat that has monopolized her dreams for the past ten months or so." He made one of his shrugging gestures. "Therefore our interests are parallel. If Professor Clarneau approves the paintings—or perhaps I should say, *when* Professor Clarneau approves the paintings— he will be able to hand you a check on the spot. He is my partner in this transaction, and the money is in our joint account, so that you can have your payment immediately, without my having to be around. I shall countersign the check when I meet him now, and he can take the paintings with him back to Paris in his station wagon. Is that good enough?"

"Very good," Annabella said contentedly.

LeGrand winked at her as he started his car's engine.

"Of course, you drove such a hard bargain that Clarneau may be shocked—but I trust you can charm him into being reconciled to the price."

"Don't even joke about such things!" Annabella remonstrated.

LeGrand was about to pull away when Simon asserted himself in the dialogue for the first time.

"Monsieur LeGrand," he said quietly. "Are you certain it was your friend who telephoned?"

LeGrand took his hand off the gear shift lever and his bushy eyebrows suddenly arched to an almost comical extreme.

"Of course it was. What do you mean?"

Annabella gave the Saint a ferocious look which clearly said, *Simon, please shut up and don't rock the boat!* but he went ahead in spite of it.

"I mean that these characters who've been so busy trying to swipe Mademoiselle Lambrini's worldly goods—not to mention Mademoiselle Lambrini—might just have decided to try another angle."

Annabella's beautiful red lips were compressed with exasperation, and LeGrand looked more impatient than worried.

"What angle?" he asked. "What would they have to do with Paul Clarneau? Are you suggesting that he . . . No. That is impossible. He has been my friend since we were boys!"

"I'm not suggesting anything—and certainly not that your chum Clarneau is a crook. I'm just wondering whether or not somebody might be using him as bait for a trap that you're about to drive right into."

LeGrand gave a nasal snorting laugh and shook his head as he put the car in gear.

"Apparently you read too many crime stories, Monsieur Templar— or live too many. You can't believe an ordinary automobile breakdown when you hear about one." He gunned the engine, then looked at the Saint again sardonically. "Of course if you would like to come along to protect me, or to protect Mademoiselle Lambrini's interests . . ."

Annabella firmly caught Simon's arm and held him close beside her.

"He can protect my interests quite well enough by staying here," she said. "Just hurry, please, and send your friend along as soon as possible."

"*A votre service!*" LeGrand said, with mock humility. His car's wheels threw up gravel. "And don't let Monsieur Templar dream up any ghosts to steal our paintings before Clarneau comes to take them!"

6

Twenty-five minutes after Marcel LeGrand had driven away, an American station wagon of venerable vintage crunched up the drive and stopped at the front door. Simon and Annabella went outside, and the driver of the car all but ran to meet them. He was a small elderly man, but powerfully knobby, with the look of one who ate little and trotted two miles every day before breakfast.

"I am so sorry, *Mademoiselle, Monsieur!*" he cried. "The gods would of course do such a thing to me on this day!"

Simon shook his hand and Annabella protested that automobile trouble was nobody's fault.

"She is old but usually dependable," the man said. "In my work I need the space for carrying paintings and statues from place to place." He suddenly stopped himself. "But I have not even introduced myself! I am Professor Paul Clarneau."

"We guessed," the Saint said.

"Do come in," Annabella Lambrini urged him. "The paintings are only a few minutes older, after all."

"Of course!"

Simon followed them into the front room and watched as Clarneau went into similar ecstasies to those of LeGrand.

"I assure you they are genuine," Annabella said. "But you are welcome to make whatever tests you have to do in order to check."

"I would not for a moment doubt your word," Professor Clarneau replied gallantly. "If you don't mind, though, I shall look more closely . . ."

He waited with eyebrows raised, until Annabella had given him her go-ahead. Then, blinking rapidly, as if the blink were an essential part of his investigatory technique, the little man began to crawl around on the floor peering at parts of the canvases through a magnifying glass, studying the surface of the paint at various angles, and inspecting the backs of the frames. After a few minutes, during which Annabella was speechless with suspense, he scrambled back to his feet.

"*Voila,*" he said happily. "It is done. They are beautiful—beautifully genuine!"

Annabella broke into a broad smile and then tried to maintain it as the Saint put in a comment.

"I thought you had to use X-rays and chemical analysis and all that sort of thing."

Clarneau answered indulgently.

"Only when my own opinion is doubtful," he said. "In this case I am quite satisfied. A person who has devoted his life to art develops an instinct for true masterpieces. Chemicals have been wrong. When my eye is convinced, it has never been mistaken."

"I'm very happy for both of you then," Simon said to him and Annabella. "Shall we start the celebration?"

"After I have something to celebrate," Annabella answered.

Clarneau looked blank. Then his face brightened.

"Oh, yes! The money." He reached into his coat pocket. "I have here a check for the amount you agreed on with LeGrand. He has already signed it, and I shall countersign it as soon as you have signed the bill of sale. You will want to read it, of course. It's rather long, but it simply says that for the amount we pay you, you agree to assign us all rights to the paintings. LeGrand and I have already put our names at the proper place."

He handed Annabella a long and closely printed piece of paper.

"While I read it I'll have Hans pack the paintings for you," she told him.

"You have crates?" he asked.

"I have a large container that holds all five," she said.

"I'll help Hans," Simon suggested.

"Wonderful. He knows where the crate is. He'll be in back—through that door—somewhere."

Simon carefully picked up one of the paintings and carried it away toward the back of the house. As Annabella read the bill of sale he and Hans appeared at intervals until all five of the paintings had been removed. Then Simon came back once more into the living room.

"Would you like to look at the crate before we put the cover on, Professor?" he asked.

Clarneau shrugged as if to say it was not necessary, but followed the Saint to the rear of the house anyway. The wooden crate was in a storage room which otherwise contained only a large cupboard, and the mysterious assortment of old boxes, cartons, battered trunks and valises, and all the other aging junk which irresistibly accumulates in such limbos. The crate was about four feet high, the same in width, and three feet deep—large enough for what the Saint had in mind.

Clarneau looked at it, satisfied himself that the five paintings had been slipped properly into their slots, where they were held by padded channels at the top and bottom, and said he was well pleased.

"Good," Simon said as the Professor went back to the living room. "Let's get this end nailed on, then, Hans."

"I had a hammer here," the chauffeur said. "I am sure I did."

"I haven't seen it," the Saint told him, untruthfully, having surreptitiously spirited it into his own hip pocket.

"Strange. I have another in the garage. I come back in a moment." Hans left the room and the Saint immediately slid every painting out of the packing crate and into the cupboard by the wall. He worked quickly but efficiently, not making a sound as he listened for approaching footsteps. The cupboard door creaked slightly as he closed it, but not loudly enough to be heard in the front part of the house. With the paintings out of sight he dumped books from one of the dusty boxes into the crate until it held the approximate equivalent in weight of the paintings.

When Hans Kraus came back into the storage room with a hammer, Simon was just fitting the end cover onto the packing case.

"I'll hold," he said. "You hammer."

Hans began banging away.

"Not too many nails—and not too hard," Simon said. "You don't want to jar the paint off the canvases."

Hans looked concerned and finished the job with a nail at each corner.

"*Gut?*" he said with satisfaction.

"*Sehr gut,*" Simon agreed. "Let's get it into the station wagon."

Hans put down the hammer and took one end of the crate; Simon picked up the other.

"Heave," he said, and they carried the crate out of a back door, around the house, and to the front door.

"Shall we put it in?" Hans asked.

"By all means. Let's give the customer his money's worth," the Saint said.

He opened the back of the station wagon and helped Hans shove the crate inside.

"All right," he said. "You can tell them it's ready to go."

Hans nodded and went into the house. Simon knew and had counted on the fact that the station wagon was not visible from the front room where Annabella and her customer were completing their transaction. Without a wasted motion the Saint jumped into the station wagon, closed the rear door behind him, and jerked the hammer from his pocket. In a few seconds he had loosened the end cover from the crate. He pulled it away and bent and flattened the bared nail points into the pinewood of the cover. Then he climbed into the crate himself, kneeling on the books, and tapped a pair of nails into the inner side of the cover so that he could use them as handles to pull the cover snugly into place. It was a simple matter then to secure the cover with another couple of nails driven lightly at an angle from inside.

Enough light came through minor crevices of the box to enable the Saint to see his own hands as his eyes adjusted themselves. He had had to work blindly while fixing the cover in place. Now he settled back in comfort in a sitting position, leaning his back against the rough inner wood of the container with his long legs only moderately cramped.

He waited and listened, and in a very few minutes he heard voices approaching the station wagon.

"I really don't know," Annabella was saying. "Hans said he was out here."

"Well, if you don't mind, I must be on my way without saying goodbye to him," Professor Clarneau said. "LeGrand will be waiting anxiously for me."

The rest of the conversational interchange was largely drowned by the opening and closing of the car door and the starting of the engine. As the station wagon pulled away Simon heard only one phrase shouted merrily by the driver:

"Don't drink too much champagne before lunch!"

The station wagon lurched out of the driveway and onto the road, but it did not turn toward the main Paris road. It turned right instead. The Saint could tell that much by centrifugal pressures even though he could see almost nothing through the tiny crevices in the crate. But presently instead of continuing in its original direction the station wagon made another right turn. It seemed to Simon that it was heading toward Paris all right, but by a devious route.

He relaxed. The noontime sun sent slivers of light across his hands folded on his knees. The vibrating wooden box, shaking rhythmically now and then, had a soporific effect that made him as drowsy as if he had been at home in bed. Up in the front seat of the station wagon the driver was whistling, and the off-key strains of *Funiculi Funicula* blended with the rush of warm air blowing back through the open windows.

The ride was not a short one. The Saint calculated that he must be in the southern outskirts of Paris proper before the station wagon slowed almost to a halt, made a gingerly bumpy turn, and honked its horn.

Simon heard a large door scrape across concrete, and the wagon moved ahead again for a short distance.

"You got them?" somebody shouted in Austrian-accented German.

The driver answered in foreigner's German which might have had somewhat garlicky Neapolitan flavor: "Of course! It went like clockwork. Where is the trunk?"

"Upstairs."

The driver got out of the station wagon and slammed the door hard.

"Then let's get it down *here*, shall we?" he said impatiently.

Simon heard the two pairs of footsteps moving away. After a few seconds he took his hammer and pulled out the two nails which held the end of the wooden crate in place. In a moment he had pushed it open far enough to allow him to look at his surroundings.

He was inside some sort of garage or small warehouse which had no windows. Next to the station wagon was an old Volkswagen bus. There was assorted automotive junk scattered around the place, none of it worth noticing twice. The Saint rolled quickly out of the crate and replaced its cover, tacking it into place with four efficient blows of his hammer. He was just getting out of the back of the station wagon when he heard someone coming down a flight of stairs at the rear of the garage. Simon ducked and waited, peering around the corner of the wagon until he had ascertained that the intruder was alone. The man was, in fact, so preoccupied with not dropping a tray he was carrying that he would not have noticed the Saint if he had been standing bolt upright. Simon recognized him as one of the two characters who had put Hans Kraus to sleep and tried to kidnap Annabella Lambrini outside LeGrand's gallery the day before.

The man with the tray opened a door on the left side of the garage, beyond the Volkswagen bus, and kicked it shut behind him. Simon followed stealthily, crossing the greasy floor of the garage, after a backward glance to make certain he had left the station wagon closed, and gently opened the door which the man ahead of him had entered. It led down a short passage, at the end of which was another door, much stouter than the first. It was half open, and the Saint could hear a low-pitched voice speaking bad French.

"Here is to eat."

It was Marcel LeGrand's voice which answered.

"We don't want food! When are you going to let us out of here?"

Another male voice, unknown to Simon, joined in.

"This is an outrage! You can't get away with this!"

"Be quiet! I untie only your hands so you eat."

The Saint slipped quietly through the door into the small dank room. The man who had been carrying the tray was bending over Marcel LeGrand, who was tied in a straight chair. Next to him, bound in another chair, was a thin white-haired man who would undoubtedly turn out to be the real Professor Clarneau.

LeGrand's startled expression betrayed Simon's entrance. The captor turned and met the edge of the Saint's hand. The chop descended with the force of an axe, and sent its victim sprawling unconscious on the stone floor.

"Monsieur Templar!" LeGrand cried. "Wonderful! How . . ."

"Quietly!" Simon cautioned him, untying his hands. "Are you all right?"

"Yes, but how did you know we were here? This is my friend Clarneau. They stopped his car. They made me sign a check . . ."

"I can imagine," the Saint said. "We can talk later. For now, get out of here through the window in the passageway between here and the garage. Hurry!"

Professor Clarneau, who looked like a large white rat in an old-fashioned black suit, was opening and closing his mouth without making any noise. For that hysterical silence Simon was grateful.

"I want you to get the police. Tell them to come grab these boys as fast as they can."

He and LeGrand hoisted Clarneau, who was still opening and closing his mouth, out of the passageway window. The Saint then had to boost LeGrand's ample bulk out unaided, and it was fortunate that he had the muscle for the job.

"Aren't you coming?" LeGrand asked Simon from outside.

"No. I have some work to finish up here. Go get the police, then go straight home and stay there. I'll see you there tonight—and have your check book ready if you still want to become the world's most envied art dealer."

7

Simon waited until he could no longer hear them moving away, and then went very quietly back to the door which led into the garage. It was half open, and through the opening he could see two men just arriving at the bottom of the stairs carrying a large trunk. One was the driver of the station wagon who had impersonated Clarneau, and the other was recognizable as the second member of the previous day's unsuccessful kidnap team—it seemed to Simon that if they were going to keep coming back into the action he would need to think of them in some less cumbersome way, and decided to call them Tweedledum and Tweedledee.

He used the Volkswagen bus as cover to slip through the doorway and get nearer. In his hand was a gun he had taken from the pocket of Tweedledum in the room behind him.

"We'll have to remove the frames in order to fit the things into this false bottom," said the Clarneau impostor, as they put down the trunk at the rear of the station wagon. "But it is worth the trouble, I assure you. No customs man would think of looking."

"And no policeman, I hope."

"Don't worry. By the time the police know anything about this we'll be over the border and halfway home."

They began to drag the wooden crate from the back of the station wagon.

"Where is that dunce, Gunter?" the substitute Clarneau wondered aloud. "Feeding LeGrand with a silver spoon?"

"This doesn't weigh much, does it?" said Tweedledee.

"Canvas is light. And yet it's worth a hundred times more than solid gold."

There was a creak of nails being tugged from wood, and then stunned silence.

"Disappointing, isn't it?"

The two men whirled to face the voice. It belonged to the Saint, who was standing behind them on the safe side of a black automatic. Tweedledee made a sudden move, and Simon sent a shot through the edge of his coat sleeve. There were no more movements, sudden or otherwise.

"I know it's disappointing," he murmured. "You expected a Madonna or two, but you'll just have to make do with one Saint."

He relieved Tweedledee of another pistol, checked the fake Clarneau, and backed away again.

"How . . . did you get here?" the smaller man asked him.

"I was breathing down your neck all the way. Now why don't you tell me how and why you got here?"

"We tell you nothing."

"Well then," Simon said, "lead the way to the dungeon, please."

He indicated the way with the nose of his gun and followed them down the passage to the room where they had held LeGrand and the real Clarneau prisoner. Tweedledum was still on the floor.

"He's killed Gunter!" the fake Clarneau cried in a panic.

"Not quite, I think," said the Saint. "But that can always be remedied. I do sometimes get homicidal when people try to keep secrets from me. Now just wait here and think what I might do to you if you don't come up with a good honest chunk of autobiography in the next forty seconds. I'll be right back."

He backed into the passageway and locked the door of the small room. Then he froze. Coming through from the garage were two more men. One of them, tall and black-haired, was the detective who had visited LeGrand's gallery the day before. He was smiling.

"You remember me, Monsieur Templar? Inspector Mathieu."

"I do remember," Simon said without relaxing his ready grip on the automatic.

Inspector Mathieu continued to smile as he nodded at the gun.

"Taking the law into your own hands?"

"Nobody else seemed to be taking care of it," the Saint said mildly.

"We have been watching this building," Mathieu said. "Your friend LeGrand and another fellow came running out in a state of shock and told us you were in here."

The Saint's muscles untensed slightly. But his main reaction to Mathieu, which must have been subconsciously developing since the first time he met him, was one of spontaneous and unaccountable distrust.

"Where's LeGrand now?" he asked.

"We sent him home. He was shaking like jelly. And where is the man who impersonated Clarneau?"

"Right through that door. And since I'm being so cooperative, maybe you'd tell me exactly what kind of mischief this cast of thousands is up to."

Mathieu shrugged.

"A simple case of thieves falling out."

"I hadn't noticed any falling out," Simon responded.

"The girl on one side, these people on the other."

Mathieu stepped forward with a business-like air toward the door behind which the Saint's three captives were locked. The key was already in Simon's pocket. The automatic was still in his hand. With the most subtle kind of movement he placed himself in the passage in just such a way that Inspector Mathieu could not get by.

"You're including Annabella Lambrini among the thieves," Simon said questioningly.

His piercing, dangerous blue eyes met Mathieu's dark ones, which gave way and pretended to glance around the bare corridor with official interest.

"She is not Annabella Lambrini, for a start," Mathieu said. "She's no more Italian than I am . . ." He hesitated and nervously indicated the locked doorway behind the Saint. "You're sure those men are in there—securely? I don't want to stand here talking while half the gang gets away."

"They're as harmless as three blind mice," the Saint assured him. "Tell me more."

"This so-called Annabella Lambrini is really Austrian," Mathieu said. "Her name is Anna Lenscher, and she is responsible for . . ."

Mathieu suddenly stopped again. His expression had switched from the complacency of superior knowledge to worry.

"Yes?" Simon prompted.

"Where *are* the paintings?" Mathieu asked. "We saw an empty crate out there as we came in."

"There's a trunk with a false bottom near it," the Saint told him.

"Ah, a false bottom," Mathieu said. "Clever. Shall we go and have a look?"

He pushed past his unintroduced and unspeaking assistant and led the way back into the garage. Simon followed both of them to the door through which the passage led into the garage.

"But the paintings aren't in there either," he said.

Mathieu turned from the trunk, looking plainly irritated.

"*Alors, M'sieur,* you will be so kind as to tell me where they are."

Simon shook his head pleasantly.

"I'm afraid I can't tell you that."

Mathieu, for the first time, seemed to be losing his self-possession.

"You don't know?" he demanded.

"I didn't say I didn't know," Simon answered. "I said I couldn't tell you. But maybe we could trade stories. You tell me more about Annabella, and I'll consider telling you about the paintings—if I know anything."

"Mr Templar! You are being difficult!"

The Saint would never have suffered the indignity of being taken off guard if his captives had not chosen that moment to set up a loud banging on the door of their cell. In the first second of the noise Simon's attention was divided among Mathieu, his assistant who was standing nearby on his right, and the noise at the other end of the passageway. In that instant of time the Saint, thinking in three directions at once, was as nearly vulnerable as he was ever likely to be.

Mathieu's assistant leaped forward, and Simon—who even at that crucial point had time to reflect that it might be unwise to kill a policeman, if Mathieu's assistant really was a policeman—half whirled to snap off a shot at the man's leg. He sensed rather than saw Mathieu hurl something at him as his head was turned. His skull was jarred as the flying object hit him, and darkness, like rising black water, filled his vision.

8

Annabella Lambrini—or Anna Lenscher, depending on whose story the reader chooses to accept—was at the least highly puzzled when she realized that her protector and overnight guest, Simon Templar, had vanished from her house simultaneously with the removal of her paintings.

Any strictly materialistic worries she might have had about the crated masterpieces were assuaged by her possession of a check for a very large amount of money signed by Marcel LeGrand and his expert friend Professor Clarneau. If the Saint, piratical character that he was reputed to be, chivalrously chose to steal the paintings from Messieurs LeGrand and Clarneau rather than from a lady, she could only be grateful for such old-world consideration. But her feminine pride was hurt that he could have walked out and left her—for whatever mysterious reason—without even saying goodbye.

However, she had more practical matters to occupy her mind. She had no wish to put off her dream of a California palace any longer than was absolutely necessary. She had already made arrangements for the closing of her house, and she set Hans to work packing her luggage while she had lunch.

About an hour later the chauffeur called to her from upstairs.

"*Fräulein!* Somebody comes!"

"Is it the Saint?" she called back. And excitedly answering her own question: "He must have done whatever he went to do."

She ran to the door and opened it as a green Renault pulled up in the driveway. There were two men in it, and she immediately realized to her disappointment that neither was Simon.

The tallest of the men approached her. His shorter companion limped more slowly behind him.

"Mademoiselle Lambrini, I am Inspector Mathieu. My identification."

"The police?" Annabella asked in a controlled voice.

"Yes. May we come in? Thank you."

He stepped into the entrance hall without waiting for a reply, and she followed him.

"I must ask you . . ." she began.

"You were visited by Monsieur LeGrand and Professor Clarneau this morning?" Mathieu asked.

"That is true."

"And you sold them some paintings?"

"Yes. Is something the matter?"

"I regret to tell you that Professor Clarneau was murdered today after leaving your house," Mathieu said heavily.

"Murdered!"

"He was killed in his car on a lonely country road. And the paintings were gone."

"Stolen?" she asked dazedly.

"The crate was empty."

"Then . . ."

"Then what?" Mathieu asked as Annabella's voice trailed off.

"I have enemies who were after the paintings. Men who tried to kidnap me yesterday and came onto my property here yesterday evening. They must have killed him."

"No, *Mademoiselle*. We have arrested the man who killed him. He has confessed."

"Who?" Annabella asked breathlessly.

"His name is Simon Templar."

Annabella's face was drained of color and she did not say a word in response, so Mathieu continued.

"He was unlucky. The murder was witnessed by some woodsmen who followed him. He did not give up without a struggle. He shot my colleague, Sergeant Bernard here, in the leg."

"Then you must have found the paintings."

"No. According to Templar he never put the paintings in the car."

Hans Kraus had come silently into the hallway and was listening. Now he interrupted.

"That is wrong. I helped him put the paintings into the box and into the automobile," he said.

"I am sorry," Mathieu said. "He denies that. He says he hid them here. We must at least try to confirm or disprove his story. You will not object if we search, *Mademoiselle*?"

"Not in the least," Annabella said. "Look anywhere you wish. You will not find them."

"Thank you," Mathieu said with a slight bow. "Where were the paintings last seen in the house?"

"Show them, Hans."

As Hans left the hall with the men his mutterings were clearly audible.

"A thousand times I tell her! Never trust strangers!"

Annabella stood in a kind of stupefied trance, and within thirty seconds, before she could rouse herself to any clear thinking, there was a call from the rear of the house.

"*Mademoiselle!* We have found them!"

She met Mathieu, his assistant, and Hans in the living room. Hans was carrying one of the da Vincis in front of him as if it were a gigantic cold fish he had just discovered in his bed.

"But, *Fräulein,*" he was intoning, "it is not possible. I put them in the box myself . . ."

"I am afraid that you were dealing with something of a magician," Mathieu said. "This man Templar is not called the Saint for no reason, you know. He has shown, until now, some almost supernatural qualities. It takes experts to deal with him."

Annabella did not find Mathieu's smugness tolerable.

"Then deal with him," she said snappishly, "and please leave me alone."

All she could think of at the moment was the check in her purse on the mantelpiece. Would it be stopped now that one of the men who had signed it had been murdered? And yet she had a signed bill of sale.

"You should be glad that your property is safe, *Mademoiselle,*" Mathieu was saying. "Another dealer will be glad to buy them."

"Thank you," Annabella said flatly.

"Very well," Mathieu said crisply. "Bernard, the other paintings, please. Put them in the back of the car."

"*What?*" Annabella cried, coming to life like a lighted rocket. "What are you talking about?"

"I am taking these pictures into police custody," Mathieu said with official dignity.

"But they're *mine!*"

"I am afraid they are not, *Mademoiselle.* You sold them, remember?"

"Not to you," the woman said. "There is no reason for this."

"A murder has been committed for these paintings," Mathieu said. "There are unanswered questions. I will give you a receipt. You can discuss who is to reclaim the paintings when the time comes. But for the moment you can comfort yourself that they will be absolutely safe at the Sûreté."

"My God, this is too much!" Annabella exclaimed, turning her back and raising her hands to the heavens in a pantomime of utter despair.

"Into the car," Mathieu said to his associate. "Cover them well with the car rug."

"They are very large," Bernard responded, "Can they be taken out of their frames?"

"Out of their frames?" Annabella cried almost incoherently. "Here? *My* paintings?"

"They are very large," shrugged Bernard. "We do not need the frames."

"So nice of you to leave me something," Annabella said with livid sarcasm.

"Very well, we shall leave the frames," Mathieu said callously. He gestured toward the storage room at the rear of the house. "After you, Bernard."

Hans was blocking the door which led to the storage room, clutching the painting he held as tightly as he could.

"*Fräulein?*" he asked desperately.

"Let them go," Annabella said with a weary wave of her hand. "The paintings are not ours any longer—and these are the noble police, after all. They go where they please."

"Your pardon, *Mademoiselle*," Mathieu said. "I shall help Bernard if you will excuse me."

"I believe that I can exist in my living room without you," Annabella said.

She waited, pacing the floor and occasionally coming to rest briefly on a chair, drumming her fingers on a polished table top. She could hear the tapping of hammers in the back of her house and the rear door opening and closing several times, but she could not see the men carrying the de-framed paintings into their car since it was parked out of the field of view of the living room window. Wild schemes whirled through her head like tornadoes dipping down from the clouds and then rising up again and disappearing, coming to nothing. She could do nothing but wait.

After fifteen minutes Mathieu, Bernard, and Hans, who had been hovering helplessly around the other two men like a toothless watchdog, came emptyhanded into the living room.

"All done?" Annabella asked sweetly. "Would you like the furniture now?"

"There is no point in feeling offended, *Mademoiselle*," Mathieu said. "No one is doing anything to you or accusing you of anything."

His tone implied that she just might find herself accused of something if the police decided to get nasty.

"I'm not offended," she said icily. "I am disgusted with this whole affair. The sooner I see the end of this business the happier I'll be."

"*Au revoir*, then," said Mathieu with a slight bow.

"My receipt," she reminded him.

"Oh, yes, of course."

Mathieu felt in his jacket pockets, and apparently found nothing usable after a lengthy search. Annabella finally produced a pen from her purse.

"Very efficient, you police," she said as she handed it to him.

"Thank you, *Mademoiselle*," Mathieu said, "and now . . . have you any paper?"

Annabella sighed and sat down.

"Would you find them some paper, Hans? They are so busy protecting citizen's property by carrying it away with them that they rarely have time for writing."

Hans got the paper and Mathieu found a seat at a table. He wrote and handed the result to Annabella.

"*From Mademoiselle Lambrini, paintings,*" she read. "*H. Mathieu, Inspector.*"

She threw the paper down in front of him on the table.

"Do you take me for an idiot?" she demanded angrily. "Describe them. Name the painters!"

Mathieu sighed and pushed the paper back in her direction, offering her the pen.

"You describe them, *Mademoiselle*. I shall sign."

She wrote a list, Mathieu and Bernard checked her description of the confiscated paintings, and then Mathieu signed the paper again. Annabella took it, folded it, and clutched it tightly.

"Now go," she said rudely.

Mathieu and Bernard walked to the front door.

"You are staying here, I assume?" Mathieu said. "We may need you when we bring the formal charge against Monsieur Templar. You will be available?"

"Of course," she lied. Then her voice softened and became less self-assured. "Templar . . . is he hurt? Was he shot?"

"No," said Mathieu. "He is as healthy and arrogant as always."

She nodded. Mathieu and Bernard made stiffly formal parting bows and left the house for their car.

Annabella closed the door and walked dejectedly to the living room. Hans was watching her.

"I am sorry that you had to learn this lesson," he said hesitantly.

"You're right, Hans. I'll never trust anybody again. I promise!"

"Not even your old friends?" asked a third and entirely different voice.

Annabella gave a little shriek and whirled to face the other end of the room. There stood an impeccable and nonchalant Simon Templar, not a hair of his handsome head out of place, more cheerfully arrogant and healthy than the man who called himself Inspector Mathieu could have imagined in his most fearful dreams.

9

"Simon!"

Annabella's cry was a crazy mixture of relief and horror. The latter emotion at first had the upper hand.

"You . . . you killer!" she said. "How did you escape?"

She whirled to look out of the front window in time to see Mathieu's car racing down the drive among the trees. In only a second or two it was out of sight.

Hans grabbed up a poker from beside the fireplace and put himself between the Saint and Annabella. He held the poker like a ready axe in front of him, and his hands were white and trembling. The Saint smiled at him with unperturbed amiability.

"I assure you that you're both getting yourselves worked up for no reason," he said quietly. "You were in much worse danger just a few minutes ago."

"You killed a man!" Annabella said.

"You killed the professor!" Hans joined in, bracing his legs and his makeshift battleaxe defensively.

"I've killed a number of men," said the Saint calmly, "but I haven't killed anyone this morning, and Professor Clarneau is as much alive as we are. The man who came here and took the paintings, or thought he did, wasn't Clarneau, of course."

"You're completely insane," Annabella said. "You're not making any sense."

"It's the gospel," Simon said.

"But the police. The Inspector told me himself . . ."

"He wasn't a real Inspector, either."

"What?"

"A fake cop. This Mathieu is about as close to being a policeman as I am, which is about as far as you can get."

"But I gave him the paintings!" Annabella almost shrieked.

"Then you're a very silly girl."

Whatever Mediterranean strains Annabella's pedigree included went suddenly on full power. She clenched her teeth, whirled completely around, shook both fists at Simon, and with an explosive shudder began to scream at him.

"This is your fault! All of it! You idiot! You traitor! You're behind this whole thing!"

She snatched up a vase of roses from one of the tables and hurled it at him, spilling most of the water and most of the roses over the front of her dress. Simon easily avoided the vase, which smashed against the wall beyond him, and awaited the next attack.

"Fräulein!" Hans cried.

He cast an almost imploring look at the Saint, who only shrugged and dodged Annabella's new missile—a potted cactus from one of the bookshelves. It sailed harmlessly past Simon and crashed not at all harmlessly through the front window.

"What a woman, eh, Hans?" said the Saint admiringly. "When she wants fresh air she wants it *now!*"

Annabella emitted a choked whinny of fury and charged around the sofa to engage him in hand-to-hand combat, but on the way her feet got tangled up in a lamp cord and she sprawled full length on her face with her eyes just a few inches from the toes of Simon's beautifully polished shoes.

"You're better than a wrecking crew," he said, leaning down to help her up.

She shook off his hand and sat on the rug bawling.

"Oh, go away!" she sobbed. "Just leave me alone."

"All right, I will. But first I'll give you a going-away present."

Hans had simply settled on one of the chairs, the poker drooping loosely in his limp hands. He was obviously in a mild state of shock. Simon went past him into the adjoining room and came back with five large unframed pieces of canvas. He held up one of them for Annabella to see. She stared incredulously, then scrambled to her feet.

"Simon!" she gasped ecstatically. "You . . . darling!"

An instant later she had thrown her arms around his neck and was covering his face with kisses and lipstick.

"A bit changeable, aren't you?" he remarked.

"I'm so sorry! I had no idea. I thought . . . I had to blame somebody. How did you get them?"

"Mathieu and his chum put them in the back of their car and tucked a blanket around them. I just took them out again and tucked the blanket back where it was while they were saying goodbye." He interrupted her with a lifted hand as she started to speak. "I know. They may already have noticed, so let's scoot out of here and deliver these treasures to Marcel LeGrand so you can get them off your hands and I can get you off mine."

Hans, carrying two of the unframed canvases, joined them in hurrying out the back door of the house and through a gate in the wall which bordered Annabella's property. Simon also carried two paintings, and Annabella brought the fifth. The Saint had parked his car in the shelter of a clump of trees in the neighboring wooded area.

"Wait," he said abruptly. "No noise for a minute."

They listened and heard an automobile engine roaring at high speed up the drive on the other side of the wall. Simon left Annabella and Hans in his car and peeked through the gate. He could see nothing but the back and side of her house, but he could hear shouting and the pounding of fists on the front door.

Simon trotted back to his car grinning.

"The return of Inspector Mathieu," he said as he got into the driver's seat. "Hold on to your Leonardos, darling."

He rocketed off toward the main road, and if Mathieu associated the sound with his escaping prey he had no time to react before the Saint and his charges were a mile down the highway.

Hans, in the back seat, closed his eyes and heaved a sigh.

"I am too old for this," he said. "I think I go back to Linz."

Annabella looked over her shoulder at him.

"You're going to California," she bubbled. "It's over now. You can relax."

"Let's hope so," the Saint said. "We may run into a waiting line at LeGrand's. You know there are at least two batches of people even less principled than ourselves after these paintings."

"Two?" Annabella said.

Hans groaned and closed his eyes again.

"Mathieu's team and another crowd that seems to be half German and half Italian," Simon continued. "I had the international squad locked up—the ones who tried to kidnap you in Paris—but then Mathieu bopped me in the head, and when I'd worked my way out of the room he locked *me* in, they were gone. I was fully expecting them to show up at your house, too. You wouldn't have any idea who they are, of course."

"No. And who is Mathieu, really?"

"I don't know that either. But your theories should be better than mine. You know the history of the paintings—who knows about them, who might have heard about them."

He could almost feel the distance between him and Annabella widen.

"As I told you," she said almost defiantly, "I have not had much contact with my father. I know very little."

That was that. The Saint could do without the whole truth as long as he cleared his fair profit, which he expected to earn very soon now. He had a kind of permanent quiet faith that anything he really needed to know would inevitably be revealed to him, and it was possible that what he already knew about the present case was all he would ever need to know: beautiful and mysterious girl possesses valuable paintings, two competing gangs of art thieves catch up with her at the same time, but luckily the Saint is on hand to throw them all into confusion and reap his own just reward.

"Oh well," he said to get off the subject, "maybe they're just frustrated amateur actors who enjoy impersonating cops and art experts and such. We'll concentrate on getting the loot to LeGrand. It's almost six, and I haven't eaten since breakfast. Let's get something to eat and give him a call at the same time. When I left him this noon I told him to go home and I'd contact him tonight."

"When did you see him?" she asked. "You haven't told me what happened."

"I'll tell you all about it over a glass of something restorative. We're not far from Barbizon, where the Bas-Bréau does a *canard à l'ananas* that would tempt Donald Duck to become a cannibal."

"I've lost my bearings completely," Annabella said. "I feel as if we've been traveling in circles."

"We have," Simon told her. "At least, we did once. It's known amongst us professional lawbreakers as shaking the tail—assuming anybody tried to tail us. You'll have to learn to do it if you're planning to continue with this adventurous life you've been leading."

Annabella shook her head with a tired smile.

"I just want to get it over with—and carry off lots and lots of money."

Simon nodded and returned her smile without speaking or taking his eyes from the road. He doubted whether it would be that simple.

10

After he had ordered dinner, the Saint left Annabella and Hans at the table and telephoned Marcel LeGrand at his home.

"Simon!" the dealer exclaimed with relief. "I haven't heard from anyone!"

"You're lucky," the Saint informed him. "It seems that everybody you know except Professor Clarneau and possibly me is a crook. Inspector Mathieu isn't inspecting anything but ways to get his hands on your paintings."

"He's not . . . ?"

"No, he's not. I don't think he'd try keeping up the impersonation at this stage, but I thought you'd better know." The Saint paused. "He's not standing over you now, is he?"

"Of course not," LeGrand said with surprise.

"If there's anyone holding a gun on you, to make you tell me that nothing's wrong, say 'No, she's feeling perfectly well now.'"

LeGrand laughed.

"No need for codes. There's only myself and my wife here."

"Good. May we come to your house with the paintings in about a couple of hours?"

"Yes! The sooner the better."

Simon went back to the table where Annabella and Hans were waiting to begin their aperitifs. He toasted them with a dry Martini.

"LeGrand is expecting us," he said. "California or bust."

Annabella smiled as she raised her glass.

"California or bust!"

An hour and a half later, replete with pineapple-garnished duck and Rausan Segla '59, and an ethereal epilog of orange soufflé, they left the restaurant for LeGrand's home in the western suburbs of Paris.

The house, even seen in semi-darkness, was an impressive testimony to the success of art as being business. LeGrand's establishment, in spaciously landscaped grounds, made Annabella Lambrini's house seem like a cottage by comparison. As the Saint pulled his car up to the front door he noticed LeGrand's Citroën in the porte cochere. There were no other cars. If there had been it might have given warning that LeGrand had received some unfriendly visitors since Simon had called him earlier in the evening. Of course, visitors of a really dedicated undesirability would not be very likely to have left their vehicle in plain view. There was a side road beyond LeGrand's southern hedge where they might have parked inconspicuously.

"I'm still nervous," Annabella said, fidgeting with her purse.

Simon let her out of the car. Hans chose to wait.

"It's about time to stop being nervous and start celebrating—unless LeGrand's changed his mind."

Annabella looked stunned. Then she saw the Saint's teasing grin in the light that fell over LeGrand's front steps.

"Don't joke," she said. She looked over her shoulder. "Let's hurry, please, before some of those horrible people come *here*."

Simon rang the bell. Almost immediately LeGrand opened the door, extending a hand effusively to each of them over the threshold. "I'm delighted to see you," he said. "Come in, come in, please."

"I think you are as anxious as I am," Annabella said with a small smile. "Or do you always answer your door so promptly?"

They had stepped into a sumptuously carpeted and decorated entrance hall. LeGrand waved them toward an open door to the left.

"I am anxious," he said. "I must admit it. I was watching from the window."

He was as impeccably dressed as ever, even though his dark suit was more than a trifle wilted. The reception room into which he took them was as richly furnished with antiques as some state-supported seventeenth-century château.

Annabella looked around admiringly.

"But you have everything already," she said. "Are you sure you want my poor paintings?"

LeGrand did not seem able to share her rather euphoric good humor.

"Indeed I want them," he said with a chopped laugh. "Are these . . ."

He nodded toward the stack of canvases in Simon's arms, and Simon handed them to him.

"They haven't been damaged at all," the Saint assured him. "They've been through quite a few escapes today, and during one of them they had to leave their frames behind."

LeGrand was fumbling with the paintings. He propped them up against a low table, almost knocking two half empty coffee cups onto the floor.

"I think you're both jittery," Simon said as Annabella helped him catch one of the cups.

LeGrand snorted negatingly.

"Excited," he said. "Not jittery."

"Here is your check from this morning," Annabella said.

"One of the signatures was forged by the man who impersonated the professor, of course."

LeGrand took the slip of paper and crumpled it.

"Thank you. I have another for you here."

He reached into a pocket of his dark suit and produced a check for the same amount as the discarded one. Annabella took it and all but kissed it.

"I *am* rich!" she exclaimed.

"Yes, my dear, you are," LeGrand agreed. "And now, ah . . ."

He had never offered his guests seats, and he seemed trying to decide what to do with them.

"We . . . must go now, mustn't we?" Annabella said uncomfortably to Simon. "We're all very tired."

"Very tired," Simon agreed. He was intrigued by LeGrand's manner and by the two coffee cups, one of which had lipstick on its white rim. "I'm just sorry we couldn't meet your wife. Isn't she here?"

"She is having dinner with friends," LeGrand said. "She was disappointed to have to represent me there rather than to meet both of you."

"Then she's not ill any longer?" the Saint asked.

"No, she is feeling perfectly well now, thank you," the art dealer answered distinctly.

"Good. Give her our regards. And now we must go."

The Saint tried to meet LeGrand's eyes, but the dealer refused to look him in the face. He edged past Simon and Annabella in order to open the door which led to the entrance hall. His face was completely expressionless, but it had a sheen of perspiration. His two guests went past him into the hall and he followed them to the front door.

Simon shook his hand.

"I'll be seeing you again soon," he said.

"I hope so," LeGrand answered earnestly. "And you, too, *Mademoiselle.*"

"*Mademoiselle* will be on her way to California before morning if she has her way," Simon replied.

"France's loss," said LeGrand gallantly. *"Au revoir, alors."*

"Thank you, *M'sieur,*" Annabella said. "Thank you so much. *Adieu!*"

She and the Saint walked out to their car, and LeGrand's house door closed behind them. Annabella bounced into the front seat of the car, turned, and waved the check in front of Hans's nose.

"It's done!" she exulted.

"So was our dinner," said the Saint, with a ghostly patient smile. "To a turn. So it was a dead duck."

The other two must have heard him, but it could only have been at the outer surface of their awareness.

"Money!" Hans grunted, with obviously mixed emotions.

"You'll be glad I have it when you're sitting under a palm tree watching girls swim in a pool all day," Annabella consoled him.

Simon was wasting no time driving out of LeGrand's property to the street. As soon as he was around the corner he stopped and cut off the car's headlights.

"What's the matter?" Annabella asked, suddenly sobered.

"I have news for you," Simon said. "LeGrand's latest check may be as worthless as the first one you picked up."

She stared at him open-mouthed. He got out of the car, strode around, and looked in her window.

"Excuse us, Hans, but I have to have a little private discussion with your boss."

He virtually hauled a stunned Annabella out of her seat and led her to a shadowy spot a few yards away.

"What is it?" she asked shakily.

"LeGrand had visitors. Did you notice the coffee cups? Most likely he and his wife were taken by surprise. His wife was being held hostage for his co-operation in another room of the house."

"Why . . . that's something out of an old television series!" Annabella protested. "And . . . who would it be?"

"I'm not dreaming this up," Simon assured her. "LeGrand gave me a signal. Now you tell me *who* would be giving him a dastardly deal like that."

"I?"

"Yes, you, Fräulein Lenscher."

She stared. Even in the semi-darkness the Saint could see from the expression on her face that his words had hit the mark so suddenly and squarely that she was unable even to pretend innocence.

"Where did you hear that name?" she finally said weakly.

"A large bird told me. Now give me the whole truth, and nothing but the truth, or I resign and you get stuck with a stopped check."

She hesitated between fury and desperation.

"All right. Do you promise not to try to get me in trouble?"

"You're already in trouble, but I won't make it any worse—as long as I get my fair share of the profits for all the time I've spent on you . . . Never mind the indignation bit. Give me your true life story before it's too late."

She nodded and began to speak with frantic precision.

"My father was not Italian. He was Austrian, and in the army in the war. Hitler was having various paintings shipped from Italy to a big art museum he was building in Linz. My father was involved in guarding the paintings, along with some other German and Italian officers. When Italy was invaded and the Russians were advancing from the east it became obvious that the Linz museum would never be finished. Paintings were stored in salt mines for safekeeping, and also in other places."

"And your father helped himself to a few?" Simon asked.

"He thought when the collapse came that it was as well he should have them as the Russians. These particular paintings came from the collection of a friend of his—an Italian count who was killed by Communists at the end of the war and left no heirs." She paused. "You may not believe that, but it is true."

"It should be easy to check," Simon said. "But I'm less interested in your father's ethics than I am in his exploits as an art collector."

Annabella shrugged.

"I don't know all the details," she continued. "Apparently it was quite easy in the confusion at the end for his Italian friend to place some of the paintings in my father's custody. My father hid them away until it was safe for him to get them and secretly move them . . . and they ended up here in France."

Not having any evidence to contradict it, the Saint had to be content with her story. He was fairly satisfied. If not pure fact, what Annabella—or Anna Lenscher—had told him at least had coherence and plausibility.

"So there are no owners to return the paintings to, and your father left them to you?" he asked.

"Yes," she said flatly.

"Why didn't he try to sell them himself?"

"I don't know. He liked them. And he was afraid of getting in trouble, I suppose."

"That's one of his weaknesses you unfortunately didn't inherit," the Saint said drily. "Now, about something else: this mob of aspiring hijackers that's following you around with drawn pistols. Who are they?"

"I don't know. Possibly men who were with my father in the war and suspected what he had done."

"And Hans?" the Saint asked.

"He has always been with my family. He knows the truth about the paintings."

Simon felt there was no more time to spend hashing the background history. He motioned Hans to stay in the car and then took his companion by her hand and led her down the street and around the corner.

"Do you mind if I keep calling you Annabella?" he asked. "I'm used to it."

"Please do. And now . . ."

"And now look through this hedge. You see that Volkswagen bus?"

"Yes."

"It belongs to the men who kidnapped LeGrand this morning," he said softly. "Keep your eye on it. If it should leave while I'm at the house, have Hans drive my car and follow it."

"What are you going to do?" she whispered.

"What I can. Keep out of sight!"

He disappeared from her view and made his way through the cover of hedges and the deep shadow of trees until he had re-entered LeGrand's grounds and reached the side of his house. A thin blade of yellow light shone between two curtains in a side window. Putting one eye against the glass of the window, Simon could see LeGrand, a dark-haired woman who had to be LeGrand's wife, and two of the men whom he had left locked in the garage that morning before Mathieu had interfered, otherwise known as Tweedledum and Tweedledee. Tweedledum was holding a gun on LeGrand and the woman.

"Yes," he was saying in labored French. "I was with her father when he took them. It can't be denied that I, who took risks in smuggling them through Russian lines, deserve a share. And now, congratulations on your performance, Monsieur LeGrand. If your wife will join us now we will go."

LeGrand looked stunned.

"My wife?"

"A security precaution," the man with the gun said. "So that you do not call for help. She will be released when we cross the border. In the meantime, keep silent. The paintings, Gunter? Are they in the car?"

"Yes. Gino has taken them out and will lock them in the steamer trunk."

"Alone?" Tweedledum grumbled. "I don't trust him or anybody else at this stage. Bring her along, and hurry!"

Simon congratulated himself on leaving Annabella behind to watch the Volkswagen bus. There had been no one in sight in its vicinity when he and she had looked at it through the bushes. Apparently the man with the paintings had been going from the house to the bus by one route while the Saint had been going from the bus to the house by another way. He would just have to hope that Annabella could take care of any contingency in her sector while he tried to turn the tables here.

Through the slit between the curtains he saw glimpses of Marcel LeGrand's distraught face as his wife was led from the room at gunpoint. Simon stepped back from the window and hurried along the side of the house to the front, where he had just time to slip into the dark shelter of the shrubbery next to the steps before the door opened.

Madame LeGrand came out first, followed closely by Tweedledee, who was gripping her arm tightly from behind. As Tweedledum emerged from the house he turned back to speak to an invisible LeGrand.

"Stay in there and do not cause any trouble and your wife will be telephoning you in a few hours."

LeGrand's wife and Tweedledee had stopped to wait before going on down the steps to the lawn. Simon steadied himself, muscles tensed, like a cobra ready to strike. Suddenly he sprang forward, grabbing both the ankles of Madame LeGrand's guard and sweeping the man's feet out from under him. The woman half fell as the man tried to cling to her as he crashed full length onto the steps. Simon, in a continuation of the same movement that had brought the man low, yanked him by his feet entirely off the ground like a long bag of grain and banged his head forcefully against the stone treads.

Tweedledum whirled, but before he could fully realize what was happening his comrade was a crumpled casualty sprawled half in the bushes, and the Saint was launching a new attack in the form of a leap onto the steps and a fist in the tender center of the gunman's solar plexus. LeGrand joined in at the same time, hurling himself at the man's back from inside the house. His attack was unorthodox but effective: he had jumped entirely off the ground, hooked his legs around the man's waist, and was riding him with the clinging desperation of a boy on a bucking bronco.

After the Saint's blow to the stomach, however, the bronco did not have much buck left. Simon stood back and watched as the bizarre equestrian act lurched down the steps and collapsed on the ground, the would-be kidnapper emitting a bellows-like gust of breath as LeGrand's weight sandwiched him heavily against the earth.

Simon took the man's pistol, held it on him, and helped LeGrand to his feet.

"*Mon dieu*, I am grateful!" the art dealer gasped to the Saint. "How can I ever thank you enough?"

Then another voice, one which should not have been there to chime in, spoke up with quiet irony.

"And how can I?" Then the tone of the voice sharpened suddenly. "Drop the gun, Monsieur Templar!"

Simon reluctantly let the pistol slip from his fingers to the grass. He and LeGrand turned to see the man who called himself Inspector Mathieu, together with his companion Bernard, facing the group with drawn guns from the shadow of a tree ten feet away.

"So we meet the forces of law and order once again," Simon said, with exaggerated reverence in his voice.

"For the last time," Mathieu said confidently. "You have saved us a great deal of trouble by taking the fight out of these pests." He indicated the two half-conscious men on the ground with a wave of his automatic. "And now you can retire from the battle yourself. Where are . . ."

He was interrupted by an excited and innocently happy female cry. "Oh, Simon, you've got them!"

The cry was Annabella's. She had just come running around the house without noticing Mathieu and Bernard. Now she stopped with a change of expression which would have been wonderfully comical in less catastrophic circumstances, as Mathieu stepped into the light.

"Don't move, *Mademoiselle*," he ordered.

He turned again to the Saint.

"*Monsieur*," he said harshly, "there are too many women here for you to risk trifling with us. But just to salve your conscience, I shall explain that we are not thieves. I am an investigator for an agency in Milan which is seeking to recover art which disappeared from Italy during the war."

"Those are my father's paintings!" Annabella interrupted fiercely.

"He looted them," Mathieu said.

"He did *not*!"

"Never mind; they are going back where they belong."

"Assuming you're telling the truth," Simon said, "don't you think Mademoiselle Lambrini deserves something? The paintings have been in her family for almost a generation."

"That does not legalize her possession," Mathieu snapped. "But I do not have time to waste on quibbles! Tell me where the paintings are, one of you, or we shall have to twist the information out of these ladies!"

He nodded toward Annabella, and Bernard grabbed her by the wrist and pulled her toward him with one arm caught up behind her. Annabella's eyes went wide with fear, while LeGrand turned pale. The dealer cast an agonized look at his wife, and then at the Saint

"Shouldn't we . . . tell?" he asked weakly.

"We do not want to hurt the girl," Mathieu urged. "One of you will tell us shortly anyway!"

Annabella gave a hopeless sigh.

"It's my arm he'll break," she said. "If nobody else tells, I will."

LeGrand accepted the invitation to appeasement with relief. His nerves were obviously at breaking point.

"The paintings are locked in the false bottom of a trunk," he blurted.

"Where?" Mathieu asked.

"In . . . in the car of those men," LeGrand said, pointing to the dazed forms on the ground. "I don't know where it is."

"Where?" Mathieu demanded of the group in general.

"Through there—on a side road," Annabella said. "It's a Volkswagen bus."

She looked at Simon with a wretched expression of shame at her capitulation and then dropped her gaze to the ground. Mathieu noted her look with satisfaction.

"Go, Bernard," he said. "Hurry. Get them!"

His assistant ran away across the lawn into the darkness. "We may be excused now, I take it?" Simon asked politely.

"You may not," Mathieu replied. "Not until I know that you have told the truth."

There was almost a full minute of silence before Bernard came running back across the grass into the light.

"They're gone!" he panted. "I found the trunk broken open and a man knocked out on the ground. Somebody had hit him with a rock, I think."

Mathieu expelled breath furiously. He cursed the group in front of him and then he cursed the world in general. Annabella did not look ashamed any longer, nor the least bit surprised. She looked glowingly pleased.

"If you would like to have the paintings," she said to Mathieu in a sweet voice, "you can bid against Monsieur LeGrand for them."

"You have them?" Mathieu exploded.

"My chauffeur has them, and he won't be where you can find him," she answered calmly.

LeGrand sat down on the front steps of his house and cupped his chin in his hands with his elbows resting on his knees.

"I am not bidding on anything," he muttered heavily. "I am finished with this whole affair."

As his voice trailed off, Annabella took his check from her purse and handed it to him.

"This is no good anyway, I suppose," she said. Then she turned to the Italian. "Monsieur Mathieu," she said brightly, "do you want the paintings or do I look for another customer?"

"But you . . . you are a *thief!*" Mathieu sputtered self-righteously.

"A defect of character most of us here share," said the Saint. "Why don't you pay *Mademoiselle* half the paintings' market value as established by Monsieur LeGrand? That takes into account the obvious fact that neither of you can really believe a word the other says, and that both of you will be lucky to get out of this without ending up in jail."

Mathieu pressed his lips together grimly as he thought over the situation. He looked piercingly at Annabella, who presented a front as smooth and uncommunicative as polished crystal. He looked at Bernard, who squirmed like a vaguely guilty puppy.

"Twenty-five percent?" Mathieu growled.

"Forty percent," Annabella said firmly.

"Thirty-five," Mathieu sighed with resignation.

"It's not enough," said Annabella.

"All right!" snapped Mathieu. "Forty! When? I want to get this over with."

"The sooner the better," Annabella said delightedly. "Tonight?"

"But don't call us, we'll call you," Simon put in. "Give us a telephone number we can reach and we'll tell you when and where to come."

"Bon," Mathieu said with resignation. He indicated Tweedledum and Tweedledee on the ground. "And these creatures?"

"Have you any insecticide?" Simon asked.

Marcel LeGrand stood up in alarm.

"You can't kill them here!" he moaned.

"No one is going to kill them," Mathieu said. "We shall lock them somewhere in your house, Monsieur LeGrand, and we shall wait here until we have the telephone call from Monsieur Templar and Mademoiselle Lambrini. Rather, I shall wait here. Bernard will go for the money. Does that suit everyone?"

"Can you get it tonight?" Simon asked.

"You will take *lire*?" Mathieu asked.

"I'll take anything as long as I can spend it," Annabella replied.

"We can pay then. We can go to . . . We have sources."

"Fine," said the Saint. "We'll be in touch."

"I have the VW key," Annabella said. "Let's take it."

"All right." He walked a few yards with her and then looked back. "And if anybody follows us, the deal is off—permanently."

They hurried away through the shadows.

"He's really letting us go!" Annabella said unbelievingly.

"He's got no choice," Simon replied, taking her hand and helping her through a hedge. "Are we telling him the truth this time or is there another layer to the cake?"

"We're telling him the truth," Annabella said. "Isn't it grand? I hid and watched the Volkswagen the way you said, and two men came and put the trunk in it. When one of them was standing there alone I just walked up behind him . . ."

"And walloped him with a large chunk of native limestone?" Simon asked.

"Exactly!" Annabella beamed.

They had come to the Volkswagen bus. Annabella pointed into the bushes, where a man lay gagged and trussed.

"Did you tie him?" Simon asked.

"Hans did."

"And the paintings?"

"Hans took them in your car. I told him to go and wait for us at a park about a mile from here."

"Great work," Simon said. "Unless, of course, Hans is half way to the Himalayas by now."

"Hans would never betray me," Annabella said confidently. "Let's go."

And she was right. When Simon, following her directions, had driven along the requisite streets, he saw his car next to a small park across from a school building. Hans got out of the driver's seat only after the Saint and Annabella had stepped out of the Volkswagen and could be clearly identified by the light of a street lamp.

"Everything is good?" he enquired.

"Everything is good if you have the paintings," Simon answered.

"*Aber natürlich!* They are here, in the back seat."

Simon took out each of the paintings in turn and quickly inspected them in the lamplight. They were all there and in perfect condition.

"Hans," he said, "you're a gem. Let's call Mathieu and get this deal over with."

"There's a telephone kiosk on the corner," Annabella said eagerly. "I'll do it."

She ran away like a happy schoolgirl and Hans shook his head admiringly.

"She is a vunderful lady," he said. "Like her father. As you say, she is a chop off the old block."

"Sometimes we say a chip off the old joint," Simon murmured.

Hans wanted to know all that had happened back at Marcel LeGrand's house, so the Saint filled him in while Annabella was in the phone box. She returned to the car, where the men were standing, with a contented smile on her face.

"They'll be coming right away," she announced. "Mathieu has already sent Bernard for the money. I told them we'd wait here in the car."

"Good," said Simon. "Hans and I were discussing old English sayings while you were gone, and this situation brings to mind another one . . . about not putting all one's eggs in the same automobile."

"What do you mean?" Annabella asked.

"I mean I think I'll wait over there across the road in the shadows in case Mathieu decides that he'd prefer spending a couple of cheap bullets rather than a lot of expensive money."

"You think he doesn't intend to go through with this even now?" Annabella asked in dismay.

"I think he does," the Saint replied, "if he has to. But it won't hurt to give the ethical side of his nature a little encouragement."

He opened the door and let her into the front passenger seat of the car. Hans, at his indication, took the driver's seat.

"Just finish your transaction as fast as you can and get rid of him," Simon told them.

Annabella was groping at the dashboard of the car.

"Where is the key?" she asked. "In case . . ."

"In case you decide to leave me standing here holding an empty bag?" Simon drawled. "The ethical side of your nature needs a little encouragement, too."

He tossed the key in his hand, grinned, put it back into his pocket and strolled across the street to the dark schoolyard. There was a row of large chestnut trees along the sidewalk giving perfect concealment from the eyes of anyone on the lighted street. The Saint leaned against one of the tree trunks, folded his arms comfortably, and waited.

He did not have long to wait. Apparently Mathieu's financial resources were not only adequate but very handy. Perhaps the money had even been in his car—it was possible that Mathieu or his employers had anticipated paying for the paintings as a last resort all along. In any case, it was less than fifteen minutes until a pair of headlights flared around the corner and Mathieu's car pulled up and stopped on Simon's side of the street facing in the opposite direction to the car that was already there. Mathieu got out, leaving Bernard at the wheel. The engine remained running.

Simon watched from his hiding place, not ten paces away, as the pseudo-Inspector crossed the street. Annabella got out of the Saint's car to meet him. Mathieu opened the rear door of Simon's car and looked over the paintings. Seeming satisfied, he turned and motioned to Bernard. Bernard got out of the car with an attaché case in one hand. While he was still hidden by the car door from the view of the people across the street, he extracted a pistol from his pocket, clicked off the safety catch, and held it close to his body.

The Saint, like a fleeting shadow, was suddenly behind Bernard as he crossed the road and Mathieu's assistant felt the hard cold nose of an automatic pressed very hard against his spine.

"What a naughty boy you are, Bernard," Simon said so that all could hear. "Now show the nice people what you've got in your hand, and then drop it on the street with the safety on."

Bernard dropped his pistol onto the pavement, and the Saint picked it up. Mathieu ground his teeth and rolled his eyes in an expression which would have fitted quite well into one of Michelangelo's more dramatic renditions of the Last Judgment.

"Well," Simon said to Annabella. "What shall we do with them now?"

"I did not tell him to do that!" Mathieu protested, waving both hands at the abashed Bernard. "I swear I did not. Show them the money, you fool!"

Bernard sheepishly opened the attaché case, revealing stacks of banknotes.

"To pay you with," Mathieu said anxiously. "It is there. You can count it."

"Stand over there, Bernard, and give me the money," Simon said.

The currency was genuine. Annabella looked at it and then enquiringly at the Saint.

"What should I do?" she asked anxiously.

"I suggest you take it before it's devalued," Simon said. "And that you give the paintings to these two boobs so they'll stay off your neck once and for all."

There was a general sigh of relief, particularly on the Italian side of the parlay, and Mathieu anxiously received the paintings from Hans.

"You are going to let us go?" Mathieu asked, with an apprehensive look at Simon's gun.

"No fear, Garibaldi," Simon said. "Run along and don't come back."

"And good riddance!" Hans grunted after them in German.

The two Italians hurried into their car, slammed the doors with feverish haste, and roared away.

When they were gone Annabella sagged happily against the side of Simon's car.

"I *am* rich!" she exulted. "I'm at least a *little* rich!"

"*We* are a little rich," Simon corrected her.

He took a pile of *lire* from the glove compartment and put them into his coat pocket. Annabella's initial look of horror faded and relaxed into a smile as she took a deep breath.

"Fair enough. You've earned it." She took Hans's hand in one of hers and Simon's in the other and squeezed them both. "We've all earned it. Let's form a team. Is Reubens bringing good prices?"

"Quite," said Simon. "Why?"

"Well, darling, these Leonardos and things were just the *beginning*! There's lots more where they came from!"

Simon looked slack-jawed at Hans, who ducked his head in affirmation and smiled modestly through the pale lamplight.

THE PERSISTENT

PATRIOTS

Original Teleplay by Michael Pertwee

Adapted by Fleming Lee

1

The tropical African coastal territory of Nagawiland had, for most of its humid eons of existence, been of little interest to anyone except monkeys, insects, snakes, crocodiles, wart hogs, and an occasional party of black hunters passing through its inhospitable coastal marshes toward the high country farther inland. The few humans who settled permanently in the small area seem to have been the remnants of a tribe of headhunters who were defeated and eaten by a more powerful neighboring tribe.

Having settled a sufficiently safe distance from the scene of their forefathers' Armageddon, the Nagawi, as they called themselves (a word translated roughly as "the only real people") showed no enthusiasm for headhunting or anything else. They lived on what they could get without much effort—their treats consisting of an occasional lame wild pig or senile baboon—and carved crude obscene figures out of tree roots. Their religious exercises consisted of flagellating one another with thorn bushes and cutting off the ear lobes of all boys who managed to survive for twelve years—which by Nagawi standards of life expectancy represented early middle age. Those who survived the religious exercises went on to reproduce languidly but steadily, until by 1870, when Livingstone discovered it, the tribe had grown from its original handful to a thousand or more.

Their first mild notoriety was passed on to the outer world by European missionaries who had come there to see what could be done about the Nagawi's souls and the fact that the women wore no blouses. The missionaries reported that the Nagawi chieftains pre-chewed all food before it was passed around to honored guests. Perhaps for that reason the Christian sects never showed quite the same zeal for converting the Nagawi as they did for converting tribes with different sorts of table etiquette.

The Nagawi's second wave of fame came during the 1920s when their obscene root carvings were declared by a group of Paris-centered artists (known as *"Les Sept Emmerdants"*) to be superior to anything produced in stone by Michelangelo or in wood by Riemenschneider. The Nagawi were delighted to find they could receive valuable salt and fine cloth in exchange for trinkets that anybody with ten fingers and a sharp knife could knock out in half an hour.

But the peak of Nagawiland's popularity with the rest of the world came when the foothills of its western borders were found to be bursting with ores of minerals precious to industrialized societies. Englishmen, whose nation had controlled the area since the 1914 World War, poured into the territory. They cut a harbor into the coastline and built a city there. Other towns sprang up and grew into cities. Electrical power plants burgeoned along the Bawu River. The Nagawi tribesmen could grow relatively rich if they chose to abandon their former way of life. Other native Africans trooped across the borders seeking the wages paid by the British. Nagawiland flourished.

But things changed in Britain and elsewhere. Highly educated men declared that the British had stolen Nagawiland from the Nagawi and ought to give it back, not only with its cities and power plants, but with additional reparations to make up in some small way for the damage they had done to human rights. Politicians of a number of states claimed that what the English had done amounted not only to theft, but to exploitation of Nagawi labor. Missionaries had once praised the strides the Nagawi had made since the coming of European civilization. Now the European papers printed comparisons of the wages of Nagawi laborers with the wages of workers in Birmingham, Lille, and Milan. Pictures compared Nagawi shacks with residential areas of London and Stockholm. A Nagawi man who had been sent to Oxford to school went over to Hyde Park every Sunday morning and publicly cursed the English for sadistic brutes. The English audience applauded politely and took guilty note of the speaker's scarred neck and missing ear lobes.

The political earthquakes which followed in due course were met with determination on the part of the white population of Nagawiland to maintain their own human rights.

In the move of the area from colonial status toward independence, only one man seemed able to keep the conflicting forces in fair balance and prevent his country's becoming the slaughteryard into which so much of the rest of Africa had been turned. His name was Thomas Liskard, and he was the white Prime Minister of Nagawiland.

On a certain morning in January, Prime Minister Liskard prepared to fly to London for crucial talks with Her Majesty's government which, it was hoped, would lead to some settlement of Nagawiland's immediate problems. Nagawiland, being a small country, did not furnish its government officials with private transport planes, so the Prime Minister and his party were driven to the airport of Nagawiland's capital city to meet a commercial jetliner coming up on a Cape Town-to-London run.

It happened that on the same January morning Simon Templar was driven by taxi to the same airport in order to catch the same plane for London. The unlikely presence of that adventurer—who under his nickname of the Saint was perhaps better known throughout the world than Thomas Liskard himself—in Nagawiland is easily explained. The Saint was there as a tourist. Nagawiland is of course far from ordinary tourist routes, but then Simon Templar was far from an ordinary tourist. He was a man who lived on excitement and constant change. It was his penchant for the former which, diligently indulged from his earliest years, had enabled him to afford the latter. His buccaneering expeditions into the Never-Never Land of lawless men had earned him the fear and hatred of criminals, the grudging respect of police officials, and enough money to travel in the most elegant style anywhere in the world anytime he felt like it.

He had felt like going to Nagawiland for two primary reasons. In the first place, it was one of the few places left where one could see certain African animals in an almost completely natural state. Thanks to Liskard's predecessors, a huge preserve had been cordoned off and kept free from poachers. Simon had stayed in the guest house of the game park and thoroughly enjoyed himself for several days, luxuriating in the total absence of pressure. It was fascinating to be able to watch the animals in the park, whose lives were as direct, as cleanly instinctive and sometimes as deadly, as his own had always been.

The second reason for the Saint's choice of Nagawiland as a place to spend those few days involved a more practical kind of interest. He wanted to see for himself one of those newly emergent countries whose teething troubles provided so much grist for the world's press mills. Nagawiland had in recent months occupied considerably more space in newsprint than it did in geographical area, and much of the journalistic expanses dedicated to it were thronged with inky armies of reporters and editors marching forth in a sort of new Children's Crusade against colonialism, restricted suffrage, and Thomas Liskard. Simon Templar, on the other hand, had developed a great admiration for Thomas Liskard, without of course having had any personal contact with him. It seemed to him that Liskard was one of the few politicians in the world who was more interested in the job he was doing for his country than in his own career. His whole life reflected his ability and integrity—and it was in fact his completely unblemished reputation among the British public as well as his own people which gave him his great personal power as a statesman, and which kept his land from catastrophe.

So Simon Templar had a chance, in going to Liskard's country, not only to relax in the tropics while the world to the north shivered in wintry slush, but also to verify his positive opinions about Nagawiland's good government. It seemed to him more than ever obvious that—contrary to the strictly liberal, rigidly democratic doctrines expressed in most of the newspapers—it was slightly better that a country be governed well by a few people than that it be governed poorly by a great many.

It was not one of the Saint's intentions to take a look at Thomas Liskard himself, but the fact that he did see the Prime Minister was no great coincidence. There was only one direct flight to London each week from Nagawiland's just created jet-sized airfield, so everybody going to London in any given seven-day period would naturally collect at the terminal on the same morning.

The Saint, tall and lean and tanned, in a middleweight blue suit that tried to take into account the fact what while it was 98 degrees Fahrenheit here it would be 42 degrees in London when he got off the plane, gratefully left the sweltering glare of the asphalt drive where his taxi had dropped him, and entered the air-conditioned coolness of the terminal building. The place was not large by European standards, but it was white and clean and new, and it possessed a small restaurant which supplied him a late breakfast

When he came out into the waiting room he immediately noticed an atmosphere of expectancy among the airport personnel and the two-dozen or so waiting passengers and their friends. Simon, having read in the papers that the Prime Minister would be traveling on the same flight that he was taking, realized what the anticipation was all about. He stationed himself in a comfortable chair alongside a row of tropical flowers in colorful ceramic pots. There he could have a farewell view of the Nagawiland countryside, get a look at the Prime Minister when he arrived, and read the morning paper in detail.

The front page carried reports of threats against the Prime Minister's life by "nationalist groups," and the reassuring news that the jetliner and its passengers would be thoroughly searched for bombs and weapons before Liskard got aboard. The small but vociferous Popular Front party (which amounted to the disloyal opposition to Liskard's United Reform party, and which took a much more "liberal" line) deplored such extremist excesses as assassination attempts, but sympathized with their motives and called for Liskard's resignation and "return" of the government to the hands of "the people."

There are certain species of birds which are said to detect the approach of a hurricane several days before its arrival, and to abandon the threatened area while the air is still mild and sunny. Simon Templar had the same facility for sensing with great precision when some explosive event was about to take place in his presence. Without that sixth sense he would never have survived and prospered as long as he had. In this case he had a distinct feeling that an attempt to kill the Prime Minister would actually be made, and that if it were not made in the capital, or on the road the Prime Minister would be traveling, it would very possibly be here at Nagawiland's National Airport.

The Saint did not shrug such intuitions off lightly, but at the same time he did not regard himself as an infallible prophet. His premonition—which he was quite ready to laugh off when it proved to be wrong—took a practical form only in that it made him more alert and gave his nerves and muscles a pleasant ready tension.

"Here he comes," one of the baggage clerks said.

The people in the waiting room watched as several automobiles pulled up in the asphalt circular drive and discharged their passengers. Simon saw the tall Prime Minister's shaggy thatch of brown hair above the other heads. Policemen entered the waiting room. Some obvious secret service types already there began to look even more obvious. Then came half a dozen photographers walking backwards, and walking toward them came Thomas Liskard, his blonde wife, and his associates and aides.

A section of the waiting room had been roped off in advance, and now it was occupied by the government group. Simon, not standing and craning his neck as most of the others in the place had done, caught only glimpses of Liskard's rather rumpled gray suit in the crowd. At the same time, he saw the jet which was to take them to London swooping smoothly down onto the runway.

The photographers had just about exhausted the possibilities for pictures in the waiting room. They drifted away from the official party, most of them going out to the loading area. Some of the police went in the same direction. The pack around the Prime Minister began to break up and disperse. Liskard, his wife, and several of their group took seats in the roped-off section. The whining roar of the jetliner grew louder as the plane taxied toward the terminal building. Just before it stopped, its engines generated so much noise, even in the more or less soundproofed waiting room, that conversation came to a virtual halt.

That was when Simon Templar suddenly seemed to go mad. One moment he was lounging peaceably in his chair. The next instant he sprang to his feet with a yell, snatched up a blue ceramic pot containing a crimson tropical blossom, and hurled it across the airport waiting room at the Prime Minister of Nagawiland.

2

Within two seconds, two more ceramic pots were flying through the air from Simon Templar's side of the room toward the Prime Minister and his party. Liskard, his wife, and his associates were diving for cover, and the Saint was throwing himself down to avoid gunfire that might understandably be sent in his direction by the official party's guards. But the only gunfire came from the ceiling, and it was directed at Thomas Liskard.

Along the ceiling were a series of grid-covered air-conditioning ducts, and it was through the grating of one of those two-foot-square holes that the Saint had seen—just before he jumped to his feet, and began to throw things—the head and shoulders of a man, and a rifle barrel. Merely shouting a warning at the Prime Minister would probably have resulted in nothing more, at least for the first precious few seconds, than startled stares—even if the shout were heard at all. So the Saint threw the pots, and even before the third had smashed against the floor beside the Prime Minister's sofa, rifle shots thudded harmlessly into the sofa and shattered the plate glass window just behind it.

Before the police and the secret service men could so much as turn toward the Saint, their attention was caught by the crack of the rifle above their heads. The pistols which might have been directed at Simon were quickly aimed at the grating, and bullets clanged against the metal and plunked holes in the plaster around the hole.

There was no answering fire from the rifleman. Men dashed out of the doors of the waiting room to surround the building. Others crouched with drawn pistols behind chairs, gazing up at the row of gratings in the ceiling, waiting for more shots.

"Everybody stay down," somebody was shouting.

"Is Tom all right?" one of Liskard's aides called from the shelter of an alcove.

"I'm fine," Liskard boomed back.

His rumbling resonant voice was suited to the size of his body. He was crouched behind the sofa. His wife had disappeared entirely behind it.

"Look there!"

Since the walls of the whole waiting room were almost entirely glass, the last phase of the attempted assassination was visible to everyone inside the building. A white man in a soiled tan suit appeared on the edge of the low roof which covered the unloading area of the driveway. He fired his rifle wildly without taking real aim at any of the security men around the terminal building, then jumped to the ground. He fell forward on his hands and knees when he hit the grass, and then snatched up his rifle and ran. The guards had no choice but to shoot him down. Their weapons crackled in a sudden fusillade. The would-be assassin leaped twisting into the air, throwing his rifle above his head. Then he crashed down on the earth and moved no more.

A civilian-dressed security man and a uniformed policeman were already standing over Simon, their guns drawn. It was by no means obvious to them whether he was an accomplice of the gunman or not.

The Saint got to his feet with the utmost casualness and dusted his coat sleeves and the knees of his trousers. The secret service man looked around, not quite sure what to do with him.

"I believe this gentleman saved my life," a deep voice said.

Thomas Liskard was walking across the room toward the Saint, much to the discomfort of his bodyguard, who thought he should stay under cover until the area was declared entirely safe. The other non-official persons in the waiting room were being gently herded into one small section of the place so that they could be easily watched over and questioned. The Saint, as a man long inured to life's more spectacular possible crises, had only one really pressing thought: *Now we'll be hours late on the takeoff.*

Prime Minister Liskard strode easily up to him and offered his huge hand. He was the kind of bulky bearish man whose very clumsiness had a politically valuable magnetism to it, and whose craggily handsome face had an obvious substratum of keen intelligence.

"Thank you, sir," he said to the Saint. "That was quick thinking."

They shook hands.

"I'm sorry about the method," Simon said. "I didn't have time to observe protocol."

"I don't think there is a really proper way of telling a Prime Minister to fall on his face," Liskard replied with a grin. "I'm damned grateful."

The secret service men were standing by ready to pounce. Liskard waved them back.

"If you boys kept up on your work, you'd know who this is," Liskard said to them. "Mr Simon Templar, isn't it, unless I'm very mistaken?"

A slight raising of the Saint's eyebrows was all that betrayed his mild surprise.

"I have to admit I didn't realize my notoriety had spread quite so far," he said. "Or to such high circles."

"This is a small country, Mr Templar," Liskard said. "There's not much that happens that I don't hear about. What with constant threats against me and this country in general, we can't afford to have guests dropping in without a strict screening process—and when the guest has your fame, especially among professional policemen, his name goes straight to the top of the bureaucratic pyramid as soon as he crosses our border." Liskard smiled. "As a matter of fact, you were within our ken pretty well all the time. I have some excellent snapshots of you taking snapshots of leopards out at the park."

Then it was Simon's turn to smile.

"As a matter of fact," he said, "I have some excellent snapshots of your men taking snapshots of me. Especially a little bald chap who almost got gored by a wart hog while he was watching me watch baboons."

Prime Minister Liskard laughed out loud.

"You deserve your reputation," he said. "I hope our attention didn't offend you."

"Not at all," Simon said. "It made me feel right at home. I'd have felt a little lost without knowing that somebody was there watching."

"Well," Liskard said, "it's a good thing you were watching, Mr Templar, or I might be dead at this moment. Please do me the honor of sitting with my group on the plane."

"I'd be delighted."

An important-looking man in a dark suit came up and spoke to Liskard.

"His name was Benjamin Scott. You remember? The one who escaped from Awi Bluff a week ago."

"A madman then?" Liskard asked. "Is that all there is to it?"

"Possibly. We're putting in a call to the director at Awi Bluff. Maybe he can tell us just what sort of lunatic the fellow was."

"Is he dead?" one of Liskard's younger aides asked.

"Died instantly. Nothing on him. I think we can assume this was one insane man's big blow-up. It shouldn't have political overtones or affect your trip."

"Thank you, Stewart. Please let me know if there's anything more before we take off. I'd not like to be delayed any longer than necessary."

Stewart spoke to some other men, and within ten minutes the plane was beginning to take on passengers. Liskard was swept away, after a word of apology to Simon, in a tide of last-minute business, but a moment after the loading of the plane began, a very officious-looking young man with a bulging briefcase in one hand came scurrying up to the Saint.

"I'm Lockhart, the Prime Minister's secretary," he said. "I'm to ask you to please come past the barrier with me and join our party on the plane."

Simon turned to follow him, and almost bumped into someone else.

"And I'm the Prime Minister's wife," she said, not making the slightest move to increase the minute space between herself and Simon. "The Prime Minister didn't bother to introduce us," she went on. "I think sometimes he forgets he has a wife."

"He'd have to be terribly forgetful, in that case," replied the Saint. "But in the circumstances, I'm sure he has a lot on his mind."

She was about thirty-five, very attractive, very blonde, and there was a neurotic tension in the carefully made-up contours of her face. Simon had a hunch that her apparent calm in the midst of the storm of the assassination attempt was the result of a good deal of alcoholic insulation.

"We'd better hurry, please," Lockhart said in clipped, high cultured tones.

"Don't worry, Jimmy," Mrs Liskard said. "We won't get you in trouble with the big man."

"Shall we go on, then?" Simon suggested.

He was made considerably more uncomfortable by the boozily affectionate wives of other men than he was by wild-eyed assassins with high-powered rifles. Mrs Liskard smiled at him, took his arm before he could get it out of her reach, and walked with him around the crowd of people waiting to board the plane.

"Jimmy is a very ambitious boy," she said loudly enough for Lockhart to hear. "He's terribly afraid of upsetting the big man."

Lockhart ignored the crack and Simon tried to. They boarded the big jet and entered a curtained-off section between the pilot's area and the rest of the seating accommodations. From his window Simon could see Liskard giving solemnly confident waves to the photographers before he came up the ramp. Mrs Liskard asked Lockhart to see about getting her a gin and tonic. A steward and stewardess appeared to make certain all was in order in the private section. Mrs Liskard asked them to see about getting her a gin and tonic since Lockhart was taking so long.

Simon did not like Mrs Liskard in spite of her attractiveness. He had nothing against amiable alcoholics in general, but Mrs Liskard was too amiable to him and too unamiable to other people, toward whom she tended to take a coldly condescending attitude. And her amiability toward Simon took a curious and very irritating form of expression. When other people, such as Lockhart, were watching, she fell all over him, but when there was no one else paying any attention she dropped the whole passionate display almost entirely. Her eyes were always darting around her immediate vicinity, searching for an audience, sizing up the impression she was making.

"Here he comes," whispered the steward to the stewardess.

There was a bustle as Liskard entered the plane. Mrs Liskard went for Simon's nearest arm and hand, both her arms and hands wrapping around his like vines. She shot him a dazzling and absolutely artificial smile, which he returned as he removed his arm and hand firmly from her grasp. Her smile faded, then came back more false than ever as her husband came into the curtained compartment along with half a dozen other men. One of them was the man called Stewart, Nagawiland's Foreign Minister, who had spoken to Liskard in the terminal building about the identity of the dead gunman. Another was immediately recognizable to any reader of newspapers as Nagawiland's Deputy Prime Minister, James Todd. He was neither as dynamic as Liskard nor as vaguely aristocratic and important-looking as the fortyish Stewart. Todd was a head shorter than either Liskard or Stewart, and ten or more years older. His graying hair was thin, and he wore rimless bifocals whose thick lower crescents distorted the lower part of his eyes. He was reputed to be a professional government man of great ability, but he looked more like a village parson or almost-retired schoolteacher than second in command to Thomas Liskard.

Simon did not recognize the other four men who entered with Liskard. He judged from their deferential behavior that they held nothing like the status of Liskard and his two top associates. They stood holding briefcases and bundles of papers, while Todd and Stewart took seats. Anne Liskard caught her husband's hand as he passed her.

"Oh, Tom, we've been having the most wonderful time while you were posing out there! Except we can't get a thing to drink. Mr Templar is so fascinating. I think you should make him your second deputy or something. I'm sure *he* could handle those socialists."

Todd looked at her over his shoulder with open disgust. Liskard wore the expression of a man who had been through it all before and expected to keep on going through it. He leaned down and whispered in his wife's ear. Simon just caught his words.

"You gave me your word, if I brought you along . . ."

Mrs Liskard giggled loudly and pushed him playfully away.

"Oh, Tom, don't be so secretive!" she said with every effort to make her voice carry as far as possible. "Everybody knows you made me promise to behave myself before you'd let me come along."

"Then try behaving yourself now," Liskard said patiently.

He took a seat across the aisle.

"I *have* been," his wife protested. She turned to the Saint. "Simon, haven't I been behaving myself? Behaving means not drinking, of course." She giggled again. "I've been *trying* to behave, but Lockhart's gone off and won't bring me that gin and tonic."

She was speaking to her husband again, but he ignored her. She turned back to Simon.

"I'm really not so bad. I'm always perfectly dignified when any reporters are around, and they're the only ones who count, after all, aren't they?"

One of the jet's engines coughed and whined to full life. Simon wished heartily that he had somehow been able to warn Thomas Liskard of the assassin in the ceiling and at the same time to see that Mrs Liskard was left as a tempting target on the sofa.

"I'm afraid you'll have to let your husband judge those things," he said.

Anne Liskard's face contorted into a frowning sulkiness.

"I certainly should think a gentleman could defend me a little better than that!" she said.

Simon got to his feet as a second engine went into action.

"You're not leaving us?" Thomas Liskard said.

"With all respect," Simon answered, "I'm afraid I'm not quite enough of a diplomat to handle the problems you have here."

A lesser man than Liskard might have been gravely offended by the Saint's bluntness, gently put though it was. But the Prime Minister accepted the Saint's comment without a trace of embarrassment or irritation.

"Nonsense," he said. "Please sit down. I'm looking forward to a chat with you on the flight. My wife is just . . . overexcited. She'll calm down when she gets a drink into her."

Simon sat down again with a shrug of thanks for Liskard's understanding.

"Well, where *is* that drink?" his wife demanded of Lockhart, who came through the curtains at just that moment.

Lockhart gave the Prime Minister a questioning but otherwise absolutely neutral look.

"Would you please ask the stewardess to bring my wife a gin and tonic?" Liskard said, with quiet dignity.

"Yes, sir," said Lockhart, and turned back through the curtain.

All four of the engines had been switched on now, and their noise hindered casual conversation. Simon took a deep breath of relief as he saw that Anne Liskard had decided to sink into sullen silence. A stewardess hurried in with a double gin and tonic and profuse apologies to Mrs Liskard. The voice of another stewardess sounded from a loudspeaker in the cool blue upholstery of the ceiling in the standardized litany to which today's airline passengers have become so wearily immune that they scarcely hear it.

"Please fasten your seat belts and refrain from smoking until after take-off."

A moment later the tone of the jets changed, and the blinding white of the terminal building began to move slowly across the plane's windows. Todd turned to speak to the Prime Minister.

"It'll be good to get off the ground—and better still to get down again."

"Let's just hope it's not a question of leaving the frying pan for the fire," Liskard said good-humoredly. "From what our advance group tells me about the greeting we can expect in London, that little business in the waiting room may seem like a tea party in comparison."

3

Prime Minister Liskard's advance information about his English reception proved to be unpleasantly accurate. Even as the jet came down through the clouds to land at London Airport, one of Liskard's aides pressed his cheek to the window beside his seat and exclaimed, "Do you see that? Must be five hundred of them!"

Simon leaned across Mrs Liskard, who had been sleeping off the effects of the first half of the flight during the second half with her head resting against the outer wall of the plane, and caught a glimpse of the dark herd of human figures congregated in an open space among the terminal's complex of huge buildings. Then the momentary view was lost as the plane with strange slowness moved down an invisible incline of air toward contact with the runway.

"The welcoming committee?" Liskard asked with amused irony.

He was sitting across the aisle from the Saint, and had not been able to see.

"Your admirers seem to be out in force," Simon confirmed.

"More likely a lynch mob," Liskard responded dourly. "At least somebody cares."

The wheels of the jet screeched suddenly against the pavement of the runway, and Mrs Liskard woke up.

"Who cares about what?" she asked blearily.

Half a dozen gin and tonics had not improved her perceptions nor her appearance. Her face was puffy and her lipstick smeared at one corner of her mouth. Even so, any man with reasonable tolerance for human frailty could have spotted her as potentially one of the most attractive women he was ever likely to meet. All the more pity, Simon thought, that she should be torn apart by whatever tensions drove her into a continual desire for semi-consciousness.

"We're in London," he told her. "We were just noticing the crowd that's out to meet you."

She tried to see. The plane was taxiing in toward the passenger terminal, but was still some distance away.

"Where?" she asked.

"On the other side of that building," the Saint answered.

"Carrying roses, I suppose," she said sarcastically.

Stewart turned from his place in front.

"Possibly," he said, "but what they were carrying looked more like pitchforks."

Anne Liskard's eyes widened in a gullible expression which may or may not have been entirely put on.

"You couldn't really see that well, could you?" she asked.

Stewart shook his head, sighed, and faced front again.

"Were there really so many?" Lockhart asked. "Five hundred? The opposition must be much worse than we thought."

He was the only one of the party who seemed openly worried, but his statement sent a silent but somehow clearly perceptible wave of uneasiness through the rest of the group. The Prime Minister, who had spent the last two hours of the trip concentrating on paper work, snapped down the clasps of his briefcase.

"Let's not blow this up out of proportion," he said firmly. "These demonstrators are of no real importance. Keep that in mind. British public opinion is entirely on our side, and that's what counts. The people in most civilized countries can still tell sanity from insanity even if a lot of their politicians can't. Those howling monkeys with the placards can sound pretty bloodcurdling, but when the government gets down to business they'll think of votes."

"But these monkeys will get top play in the headlines," one of the aides put in. "When you see the papers tomorrow you'll hardly know we were here."

The Deputy Prime Minister, Todd, made an uncomplimentary and fairly obscene remark about newspapermen and the bias of the international press, which almost invariably took a dim view of self-assertive activities on the part of Europeans anywhere in the world.

"It doesn't matter," Liskard insisted. "I don't want anybody in this delegation to show any sign of disturbance, no matter what kind of demonstration they have in store for us. Is that understood? Look pleasant. Keep your dignity. It's the best way to turn one of these situations into a defeat for the other side. Remember—if out of a hundred photographs the editors can find one that makes us look bad, that's the one they'll print on the front page."

"Right," Foreign Minister Stewart said. "And the same goes for statements. I don't need to remind you that an unwise word to some interviewer could ham up the negotiations completely."

He was speaking not to Liskard, of course, but to the younger aides, and, surprisingly, to Todd, who looked grim suddenly and avoided the eyes of the other men. Apparently the Deputy Prime Minister had indiscreetly overstepped the bounds of his authority at some time in the past while dealing with the press.

"Excuse me, please," Anne Liskard said. "I must go put on a face to meet the faces that I'll meet."

"It'll be a little easier after the plane stops," said the Saint

She gave him a crisply cool smile as she stood up. She had by no means forgiven him for refusing to respond to her public displays of affection at the beginning of the trip, and then for devoting himself almost entirely to conversation with her husband during the middle hours of the flight.

"Thank you for the warning," she said in clipped tones. "I'm quite capable of lurching down the aisle to the ladies' room without any advice from Robin Hood."

Simon let her lurch and sat back down to have a look out the drizzle-beaded window. It was late in the day, and the brightness of the sky far above the earth had been abruptly exchanged, when the plane descended below the sea of clouds that had been like a solid surface beneath it, for the fading gray light of a rainy winter afternoon. The pavement glistened clammily, and east was merged with west, and north with south, in the congested sky that seemed to press down and smother the whole country as night came on.

A hundred yards away, beside one of the wings of the terminal building, he saw the wheeled stairway which would be put up to the jet's door. Near it was a black limousine and a handful of men. It was not a very spectacular reception, considering Liskard's status, and Simon regretted it. Whatever reservations he had felt about being with the Prime Minister's party at the beginning of the flight, when he had realized what sort of woman Mrs Liskard was, he had grown much more pleased with the situation during his long chat with Thomas Liskard. His intuition about the man—based only on reading—had proved right. The Prime Minister was a straight, honest, and intelligent man who shared nothing of the barren lust for power or the dependence on cloudy and utterly impractical social theories with which so many of his counterparts in other countries were leading their people in the direction of hypothetical Utopias which in reality prove to be nothing more, at their noisiest, than maelstroms of disorder, or, at their dullest, stagnant backwaters of living death. More than ever, the Saint saw Liskard as a bulwark—even if not a very powerful one—against the denial of truths about human instinct and the strange guilty deference to mediocrity, indolence, and weakness which sometimes seemed to be threatening to emasculate the whole western world.

One of the stewardesses who had been serving the party throughout the flight came into the curtained compartment as the plane stopped and cut its engines.

"We'll hold the other passengers in their places until your party is off, Mr Prime Minister," she said.

Liskard turned in his seat and shook his head. "I think it would be best if the others left first," he told her. "We might delay things at the foot of the gangway for quite a while."

The stewardess leaned down and peered out of one of the windows.

"I don't see any band or anything," she said.

Liskard laughed.

"You're probably remembering the reception you got when you flew some murderous little tribal dictator through here on his way to bawl out the United Nations. There'll be no brass band for the likes of us. We can count ourselves lucky that they haven't laid on a firing squad."

"Assuming they haven't," said Stewart with a wry grin.

Lockhart stood up as the plane's personnel set about opening the door and shepherding the ordinary passengers out. He pointed suddenly toward the open deck on the upper floor of the terminal building.

"Look at that!"

On the terrace, where friends of passengers were able to stand and wave to arriving and departing passengers, there was a violent commotion. Apparently a dozen or so anti-Liskard demonstrators had gone up there individually without attracting any special attention from the police. Now the demonstrators—who were of the shorn and shod variety, and were able to avoid arousing suspicion until they were ready to act—pulled rolls of paper from under their coats and unfurled them into banners with brief but clearly legible messages printed in large red letters.

"DEATH TO FASCIST LISKARD!"
"FREEDOM TODAY—NOT TOMORROW!"
"ONE MAN—ONE VOTE!"

The police obviously had been instructed to allow no demonstrations in the terminal building, an instruction with which the demonstrators disagreed with open vehemence when they were informed of it. The policemen tried to take their signs away, and there was a scuffle. One of the demonstrators sat down. Another clung to the pedestal of a coin-slot telescope with arms and legs. All began to chant so loudly that their words could be heard inside the plane as the passengers disembarked.

"Liskard out! Freedom in! Liskard out! Freedom in!"

Lockhart shook his head.

"Ugly-looking lot, aren't they?"

Liskard pretended he was referring to the very correctly dressed gentlemen grouped to meet him by the rolling stairway.

"You're speaking of the flower of the lower branches of the diplomatic corps," he said.

Lockhart's youthful face turned crimson.

"I mean the demonstrators, sir," he said stiffly.

Liskard, who was standing next to his secretary, clapped him on the shoulder.

"You take things much too seriously, Lockhart. You've got to laugh sometimes or you'll go loony. That's especially true when you look at types like that out there with the signs. They screech for peace, but they'd as soon kill you for disagreeing with them as not."

Todd grunted.

"I suppose you're planning to say *that* when you speak to the press?" he said.

Anne Liskard, who was returning down the aisle, produced a sarcastic chuckle.

"Don't be silly. Tom knows as well as anybody that honesty has its own season."

"At least I know when I'm lying and when I'm not—though we call it being diplomatic, not lying. At least when you know a man's self-interest is clearly tied with his own survival and his possessions and his people, you know where you stand with him. To me, the most potentially destructive man of all is the one who really *believes* his motives are based on universal ideals instead of what he'd call more selfish loyalties. Show me a man who claims he bases his actions on the principle that all power is evil, and that human want and inequality can be done away with, and that the world can be persuaded and legislated into eternal peace and brotherhood, and I'll show you a man who's either a liar or a fool . . . and most likely a very unstable and dangerous fool at that."

Anne Liskard sighed.

"The philosopher king," she muttered.

Simon, who had found it more interesting to listen than to intrude his own thoughts, extended his hand to Liskard.

"I'll just say thank you," he said. "I'd better get off with the rest of the common people. But I'd like to wish you luck."

"You aren't leaving us to that mob, are you?" Anne Liskard asked tauntingly.

"Mr Templar has already saved my life once today," the Prime Minister said. "I can't ask him to do it again. But I can ask him to dinner with us. Tomorrow night, Mr Templar? It won't be terribly elaborate, which means it may be a little more bearable than most of these diplomatic things."

"Please do!" Anne Liskard begged, with more sincerity than show. "You have no idea what a relief it would be to have a real person at the table along with all those marionettes."

"We might even be able to furnish you with some of that excitement you're so famous for enjoying. There could be other attempts against my life here in London."

At that moment, the last thing that Simon wanted was any further exciting involvement in international politics, and he might have refused the Prime Minister's invitation if he had had time to give it thought, but the last of the non-political passengers were descending the ramp from the door of the plane, and he hoped to make his exit as an anonymous member of the herd. Newspapers would be hawking the story of the Nagawiland assassination attempt all over the city by now, and reporters would be baying like a pack of hounds after any detail of the story and any personality involved—and particularly any personality already as fabled as the Saint. His chance of avoiding recognition was slim now, but it would be totally nil within another minute.

"Thank you very much," he said hastily. "I'd be honored to come, even without any gunfire to liven up the evening. But now I'd better get out of here."

"Come with us if you like," the Prime Minister said. "I'd certainly be delighted to introduce you to the press and publicly thank you for saving my life."

"I'm afraid that being blinded by flashbulbs and answering silly questions in a freezing rain isn't my idea of a rewarding experience," the Saint said. "I'd be much more grateful for dinner tomorrow."

Liskard grinned.

"Entirely understandable. We'll see you at Nagawi House tomorrow evening. Eight o'clock."

"Fine."

Simon shook hands with Anne Liskard, who apparently had forgiven him for not prostrating himself in helpless worship after her first attentions and was showing signs of becoming hot-eyed and clinging again.

"It was very exciting to meet you," she said.

"I haven't been bored for a minute myself," Simon told her. "Good night, and thank you."

As he hurried through the curtains toward the plane's exit, he heard Thomas Liskard's deep voice behind him.

"And now . . . out into the arena and the lions."

4

The violent night of the Prime Minister of Nagawiland's arrival at London Airport is a matter of history. The Saint learned the full story of Liskard's unofficial welcome to London by the forces of righteousness the next morning in the newspapers.

Apparently the demonstrators blocking traffic outside the terminal had been more than mildly chagrined that a would-be assassin had failed to kill Prime Minister Liskard in Nagawiland and had resolved to set things right by killing him themselves. They had not succeeded, although a window of the limousine carrying him had been cracked by a thrown brick and spattered with broken eggs. Foreign Minister Stewart had been spat upon, and Deputy Prime Minister Todd had been struck by a placard bearing the vague but undeniably optimistic sentiment, "FREEDOM AND EQUALITY FOR ALL PEOPLE!"

The Saint was surprised and gratified to read that Liskard's secretary, young Lockhart, had pushed a demonstrator to the ground who had been trying to kick the Prime Minister as he left the terminal building, and had also torn in half a colorfully if obscenely illustrated poster which read, "AFRICAN PEOPLE'S UNION WILL TIE KILLER LISKARD'S HANDS WITH HIS OWN ENTRAILS!"

Lockhart's exploit of course received top billing in the newspapers, which featured photographs of him in action along with such captions as, *"Police state Gestapo in London? Liskard's burly bodyguard attacks demonstrator."* Other photographs highlighted injuries suffered by the pickets, and showed policemen engaged in the sadistic activity of dragging them out of the public thoroughfare. "Spokesmen" seriously questioned whether representatives of a regime like Liskard's, which deliberately stirred up such commotions, should be allowed to set foot on English soil or not.

The afternoon papers headlined the news that Lockhart—who was no more burly than he was a bodyguard—had been "disciplined" by Prime Minister Liskard and sent back to Nagawiland. Simon, as sorry as he was to hear about that, understood the political necessity of Liskard's action. Without the support of the English majority, Liskard's mission would be doomed. The vicious demonstrations against him had certainly increased his popularity, while Lockhart's behavior—especially as it was reported in distorted form by the left-wing press—was just the kind of thing that could ruin Liskard completely. His position was so precarious that he and his associates would have to be a dozen times more virtuous, more polite, more modest, more unblemished in general than ordinary men to stand even a small chance of being judged the moral superiors of the most debased inmates of Her Majesty's prisons. If Liskard could pull that somewhat superhuman feat off successfully, the stability of his country might be preserved.

And that, Simon thought, was exactly what Liskard's political enemies would be most anxious to prevent. If Liskard managed to get through his stay in England without something more deeply damaging to his cause than riots or rifle bullets aimed in his direction, it would be a miracle of such magnitude that the Saint would not thereafter have been at all surprised to see the monumental stone lions of Trafalgar Square get up off their perches, yawn, and stroll away toward Piccadilly Circus.

Simon enjoyed his whimsical thought about lions as he was leaving Upper Berkeley Mews and setting out by taxi for the Prime Minister's dinner in Hampstead. He had spent the day doing those necessary and temporarily novel-seeming ordinary things which people do just after returning from a long trip.

Now he was ready to relax, and attending a formal dinner with a lot of stuffed tuxedoes was not his idea of relaxation. There was only one compensating factor. As dull as the dinner might be, it would bring him in close contact with the most important political situation developing in London at that time. There was some interest and a little excitement in that. But more to the Saint's taste was the prospect of keeping up a contact with a worthy man whose very continued existence from hour to hour was something of a marvel, and who was bound to become the target of the most advanced forms of defamation and general nastiness that his enemies could contrive.

The Saint did not like plotters against worthy men. He had devoted considerable energy in his lifetime to bringing the activities of such plotters to abrupt and often violent ends. The fact that their ends often coincided with a transfer of material assets from their coffers to the Saint's numerous bank accounts was no denial of the fact that he gained great spiritual satisfaction just from doing them in. And if he could help Thomas Liskard, if only by appearing at a dinner, he was delighted to do it.

Nagawi House was a fairly modest establishment, as residences maintained by governments on foreign soil go, but it was set back on spacious grounds, and its restrained brick lines were a tribute to neo-classicism. Fortunately its generations-dead architect had thought not only of beauty but also of practicality, having included a high brick wall which helped keep out the thieves of his own time and the picket lines of the twentieth century.

They were there, a hundred shaggy-bearded worshippers of dirt, despisers of achievement and work, fearers of all things strong and superior, proclaimers of an opiate called universal love. They were the bacteria of anarchy, and they were gathered in motley force outside the gates of Nagawi House.

"Hold your nose, sir, we're going through," the taxi driver said over his shoulder.

The cab pushed through the lane held open by hard-pressed police, and several dozen voices on either side screeched obscenities. Inside the gates, along the crescent drive, the lawn was free of wild-eyed humanity. Hoarfrost glittered on the grass in the light of lamps which stood on either side of the doorway. The doorman greeted Simon and ushered him into the entrance hall, where his identity was checked before he was admitted to the main reception room. There he took his place in the line-up of dignitaries shuffling toward Thomas Liskard and his wife.

"Simon, I'm so glad you came," Anne Liskard said smoothly.

For the first time the Saint understood why—aside from the woman's silvery beauty, which was dazzlingly set off by diamonds and a pure white shoulderless evening dress—Thomas Liskard had been able to fit her in with his political career. If she was drunk, she was concealing it gracefully. Her smile was warm and dignified, and her handshake completely decorous. Apparently she was ambitious enough or decent enough to control her weaknesses in public. If Simon had not seen her in more intimate action the day before he would never have guessed that such shattering drives were fighting beneath her entirely attractive surface.

"It's nice to see you again," the Saint answered, no less suavely. "I'm sorry you had that trouble with the pickets yesterday."

Now he could see that her smile was a little too fixed and imperturbable to be genuine.

"It was quite an adventure," she said. "You came down to Africa to see the wild animals, but I was quite surprised to discover that you have more right here than we ever dreamed of having."

"Not more," Simon said. "Just more in evidence."

He moved on to Thomas Liskard, who had just been vacated by a very large gentlemen with a white walrus mustache.

"Very happy to see you," he said, shaking Simon's hand warmly.

His smile was much more spontaneous and convincing than his wife's had been, but there was a strain in his eyes which betrayed his worry.

"I hope things are going well for you," the Saint said.

"Well enough. We don't really get down to business until tomorrow."

Liskard was obviously preoccupied with his duties as host and greeter, so Simon started to move away after a few more words. He was surprised when Liskard stopped him with a touch on his arm and leaned forward to speak to him confidentially.

"I must talk to you alone," he said. "Please don't leave after dinner before we can get together."

"Certainly."

The Saint felt that peculiar thrill which often ran through his nerves when he sensed that he was on to something out of the ordinary. Maybe he would have a chance to give Prime Minister Liskard more than moral support after all. The social chitchat and the prolonged not very good dinner became no more than a journey he had to endure until he could speak with Liskard in private.

At last the thirty guests had been sufficiently regaled with toasts, filets, and crisp conversation to warrant their exodus from the dining room back to the reception room for after-dinner drinks. It was at that point that Liskard caught Simon's eye and moved toward a hallway in the opposite direction from the movement of the crowd. The Saint followed. A moment later he found himself in an oak-paneled study—a lush but impersonal setting of leather chairs, a massive desk and heavy tables, shelves of books arranged in untouched perfection, and several paintings of Nagawiland's countryside and industrial plants.

Liskard locked the door behind Simon and thanked him for coming. The public smile had vanished from his face, which looked much older than it had the day before. He said nothing as he poured brandy from a decanter into a pair of snifters. The Saint took the wing-backed chair which the Prime Minister indicated. He warmed the brandy in its crystal sphere with his hands as he waited. Liskard unlocked a drawer of the desk with a key taken from his pocket and drew out a fat white envelope.

The Saint inhaled the scent of the cognac deeply and released his breath with profound satisfaction. It was a satisfaction produced by more than the aroma of Delamain. It was a combination of contained excitement and pleasure at the knowledge that his destiny was running on schedule. The white envelope was going to confirm his earlier thoughts about the calumnies which would be directed at Liskard. The lions would stay frozen on their pedestals in Trafalgar Square.

"This came in the mail today," Liskard said.

He did not offer the envelope to Simon, but slapped it down on top of the desk with the air of a man dealing a possible fourth ace to a gambling opponent. Simon nodded and let some brandy touch his tongue. Liskard clasped his hands behind his back and paced to the outer wall. He drew back one of the heavy drawn curtains slightly and looked out toward the front gate. The chants of the mob there came faintly into the room and faded again as he let the curtain fall back into place.

"Those are photostats of letters I wrote to a woman—a girl—here three years ago. Whoever sent them says he'll show them to my wife and to the press in two days from now."

Simon put down his glass.

"That's clear enough and to the point. What's the price?"

Liskard paced back to the desk and sat down heavily in the swivel chair behind it.

"That's the most peculiar part. There's no mention of money specifically. Look."

Liskard leaned forward and opened the white envelope. He handed the Saint a small square of note paper whose typed message Simon studied carefully.

Liskard:

You have 48 hours to think about these literary efforts of yours. Then I shall turn half of the originals over to your wife and half over to the newspapers . . . the ones which go in for big black headlines. You may be wondering what you can do to stop this from happening. Keep wondering.

Simon put the paper back on the desk.

"That's a peculiar form of blackmail. It's very possible you'll hear more from this character before the time is up. Could he have some special interest in wanting you to squirm?"

"A lot of people would like to see me squirm in a vat of hot oil or worse."

Liskard seemed to be holding something back. Rather than question the Prime Minister directly, however, Simon first mentioned another angle.

"If this is being done by political enemies—which are the most likely sort of enemies for a man in your position to have, I should think—then why didn't they just turn the letters over to the press right away without warning you? Or if they want some political concession out of you, like quitting the conference here, why didn't they hit you with that demand when they hit you with these photostats? It seems stupid to give you a chance to prepare some kind of counterattack."

"It does," agreed Liskard.

Again, he seemed reluctant to say what was on his mind, so Simon continued with the obvious conclusion.

"Whatever the ultimate point of this turns out to be, it seems right now that the motive is to make you suffer. That hints at a personal vendetta, and it may mean that whoever sent these to you has no real intention of showing them to anybody else. He just wants to give you a couple of sleepless nights."

"I'd like to think it was that easy," Liskard said.

He had slumped his big body far down in his chair and was staring at the oriental carpet with brooding eyes.

"I assume you didn't ask me in here just so you could share the glad tidings with me," the Saint said.

Liskard looked up at him.

"No. Of course not. I'm being presumptuous enough to ask for your help. By reputation, you particularly dislike blackmail. It's the sort of thing you may be willing to fight against—and I'm willing to pay you enough to make it quite worth your while."

"So far so good," said the Saint. "But I can't be much help if you don't let me know your own theories. Do you have any idea who might be doing this to you?"

Liskard sighed.

"Not really, but obviously my first thought is the girl I wrote them to. And naturally I'm not anxious to accuse somebody I . . . once thought so much of."

"If you want me to help, we can't be too delicate. What's her name and what's the whole story about her?"

"Her name is Mary Bannerman," Liskard replied after a moment's pause. "I met her here in London when I was up with the High Commission for several months. As I said, that was three years ago. She was a secretary trying to break into modeling. We had an affair that went on during most of the time I was here."

"Was your wife in London?"

"No. She stayed at home."

Simon took up his brandy glass again and got to his feet for a stroll around the room.

"And you wrote the letters while you were here? The Commission traveled all around Britain, as I recall."

"Right. She was in London, and during those times I was away I wrote the letters . . . except for a few I sent her in England after the Commission went back to Nagawiland."

"Absence didn't make the heart grow fonder, I gather."

Liskard shook his head.

"It wasn't that."

"Was it just a physical thing that didn't affect either of you very deeply?"

"I'm afraid it wasn't that either. I told her I loved her . . . as she told me. I told her I'd leave my wife and marry her . . ."

"You told her all this in writing?" Simon asked, indicating the envelope.

Liskard looked sheepishly miserable.

"Yes."

"But you didn't really mean it?"

"I meant it at the time. That's what makes me feel guilty. I had every intention of doing just as I'd said, and then . . ."

"Then what?" Simon asked when the rest of the statement failed to materialize.

Liskard looked up with a gesture of self-disgust.

"Templar, there are some things a man is almost too ashamed of to talk about. I went back to Nagawiland. Suddenly, I was in line for Prime Minister. A divorce would have ruined my chances, especially since my wife's family is very big in our politics down there. So . . . I didn't leave Anne. I dropped Mary. And I became Prime Minister."

"How did Mary Bannerman take that?" Simon asked.

"Badly, but you can't blame her, especially since she was very young."

"How young?"

"Twenty-three then."

"And married by now?"

"I honestly don't know anything about her, except that she did become a model. I've seen her picture in magazine advertisements."

Simon studied the expression on Liskard's rugged face.

"Apparently you still have some feeling for her, if you don't mind my saying so. If she is behind this, you're going to have to think of her as an enemy, and not as a poor seduced child you feel terribly guilty about."

Liskard's eyes flashed with momentary anger. Then reason took the upper hand again and he spoke with controlled emotion.

"I'd rather you hadn't said that, but . . . you do have a point. Of course my reason for not telling the police—or anybody else except you—about this isn't just because of the danger of the news leaking out. It's also because I feel Mary's partially justified in doing this, if she is doing it, and I don't want to hurt her. I'm hoping that you can—if you will—find out what she wants and somehow stop this whole business before anybody gets hurt."

"That's a little like telling me to go out and stop a charging rhino tenderly. If she's really out for revenge, what exactly *do* you expect me to do?"

"I'm sure you're better at things like that than I am," Liskard replied. "But my first thought of course is that we should find out what we can about Mary and what she's done with my letters . . . You might think of a way to get them back."

Simon compressed his lips thoughtfully.

"Are they really very compromising?"

"Compromising?" Liskard echoed. For the first time since they had entered the room his usual sense of humor showed signs of breaking through his gloom. "They're lurid. They make Casanova sound like a Salvation Army sergeant."

"May I see one?"

The Saint had no prurient interest nor any great curiosity about the intimate details of Thomas Liskard's love life, which were undoubtedly very much like the intimate details of everyone else's love life. But he had learned to be skeptical enough about guilty-conscience reactions to want to make his own impartial estimate of how much dynamite there really was in that white envelope.

Liskard hesitated, and then without saying anything opened the envelope and handed over one of the sheets of paper which it contained. Simon read it quickly and was satisfied that the Prime Minister had not exaggerated.

"I see what you mean," he said simply.

He handed it back.

"Pretty ridiculous, isn't it?" Liskard said uncomfortably.

"Pretty certain to ruin your political career if it gets out," the Saint said. "That kind of thing may go a long way with the ladies, but it doesn't go over very big with the voting public."

"You may think this is just high-sounding talk," Liskard responded with desperate earnestness, "but now it isn't my own career in politics that I'm worried about. If these negotiations should fall through, it could lead to chaos in my country."

"I agree," said the Saint. "And there's not much time. Let's see if Mary Bannerman is in the phone book."

5

Mary Bannerman's Chelsea address said a good deal for her successful rise from secretary to model. The Saint drove directly to her apartment building from Prime Minister Liskard's dinner party. Back in Hampstead the diplomatic set was still going strong on a fuel mixture of champagne and hot air, but Simon had decided to try to see Liskard's ex-girlfriend that same night—and without a preliminary phone call which could have helped her to evade his visit.

It was 10:30, and Chatterton Close—the half-block cul-de-sac in which Mary Bannerman lived—was quiet at that hour. Some very large, shiny, expensive cars and some very small, shiny, expensive cars were parked along either side of the street. The only sound was the click of the high heels of a pair of fur-wrapped girls hurrying along the sidewalk. Simon went into the three-storeyed white building marked "109" and climbed carpeted stairs to the second floor. Like the halls of all very fine apartment buildings, its halls were silent and smelled of wax and lemon furniture polish, without the slightest taint of pork fat or cabbage. Simon was pleased with that. He had a distinct preference for evildoers (if Mary Bannerman should indeed turn out to be an evildoer) who lived in sanitary surroundings.

The brass nameplate beside one of the doors read "BANNERMAN." Simon was about to ring the bell when he heard voices filtering from the other side of the door. Obviously, considering the quiet of the rest of the building, the dialogue had to be taking place at an impressive level of volume for him to be able to hear it at all. The first voice was a woman's.

"Get away from here, you filthy swine!"

"Give them to me or I'll wring your selfish little neck!"

"Just try it!"

"I will!"

On the next line the woman's voice rose to a screech of operatic proportions.

"Put away that gun, you fool!"

Simon was a great believer in the time honored equation of homes—or even apartments—with medieval castles, and concomitant rights of privacy, but he was an even stronger believer in the rights of women not to be menaced with weapons unless he was satisfied that they deserved such treatment. He turned the handle of the unlocked door and threw it open, knowing that would be enough by itself to stall any murder which might be about to take place.

The sudden opening of the door brought an even louder screech from the female voice than had the threat of the gun, and Simon found himself looking at a scene quite different from what he had expected.

The aggressive male was in a chair with a piece of paper in his hands. He looked brawny enough to do plenty of damage even without a gun, but he was much more startled than threatening. The woman was on her feet and had thrown herself back against the nearest wall in fright. She was young, redheaded, and gorgeous. The evidence that she was gorgeous was especially plentiful, since she was wearing a gauzy white negligee that might have been woven of spider webs and spun sugar, but obviously wasn't since it was standing up under a considerable strain as its wearer twisted her body to stare at the Saint.

"Madame Tussaud's?" he inquired apologetically.

The young man who had been seated jumped to his feet. He wore expensive trousers and a gray cashmere turtle-neck sweater.

"Who the hell are you?" he demanded.

"Apparently somebody who's in the process of making an ass of himself," Simon admitted. "Maybe I should go out and come in again."

"Maybe you should just go out, period!" said the girl inhospitably.

"Who is this?" the man asked her.

"How should I know?" she snapped. "Do something—don't just stand there."

Simon held his ground at the threshold and raised both hands in an appeal for understanding.

"I was about to knock," he explained, "when I heard what seemed to be very peculiar things happening in here." He looked at the man. "Were you or were you not about to shoot this beautiful young lady?"

The beautiful young lady burst out laughing.

"You heard us rehearsing?" she cried. "Oh, that's super, isn't it, Jeff?"

Jeff showed considerably less good humor than the girl.

"Very funny," he said without smiling. "And what were you doing listening at the door?"

Simon chose to ignore the provocative slant of the question and spoke directly to the girl.

"I was about to knock," he said easily. "My assumptions don't seem to be in very good working order this evening, but I assume you are Mary Bannerman."

"I am," she said. "And I assume you are Sir Galahad . . . or at least Don Quixote."

The Saint sidestepped the implied question.

"And I assume you two are rehearsing a play."

"*Were,*" said the man pointedly. "You'd . . ."

Mary Bannerman interrupted, coming from the opposite wall to interpose herself between Simon and her original guest. She showed absolutely no self-consciousness over her distractingly revealing costume.

"Not a play," she said. "A television commercial . . . for Sweetomints."

"Sweetomints?" said the Saint, as if doubtfully repeating an improper word.

Mary Bannerman pouted her lips and looked with melting green eyes into a non-existent camera.

"Don't try taking candy from *this* baby. Buy your own Sweetomints."

"Never mind," said the man called Jeff.

But Mary Bannerman ignored him.

"Right after he pulls the gun, I grab him and throw him over my head, and the whole bit ends with my sucking a Sweetomint. Of course I don't really throw him over my head, but it looks that way, and of course it's not Jeff, it's some actor. Jeff's the director."

"I see."

"Well, I *don't* see," Jeff said impatiently to the girl. "Why are you standing around jabbering to this character when he won't even tell you who he is?"

"Because this is my apartment," she came back huffily. "And . . ."

"And maybe her taste in men is improving," said the Saint.

There was every sign of an imminent explosion, but Mary Bannerman stopped it.

"Wait a minute, Jeff." She looked at Simon seriously. "If you did come to see me, you'd better tell me who you are and why you're here."

"My name is Simon Templar," he said, "and my reason for coming to see you is confidential."

He glanced meaningfully at the other man.

"Good heavens," Mary Bannerman said with a sophisticated lack of vehemence. "Simon Templar . . . the Saint. Are you kidding?"

Simon shook his head.

"Don't you see the halo?" he asked.

"No, but now that you mention it, the face is familiar."

"Saint?" the director asked blankly.

"You colonials," Mary Bannerman said to him. "You're really out of it. Haven't you ever heard of Simon Templar?"

"No."

"Fair enough," said the Saint. "I've never heard of you, either."

"This is Jeff Peterson," the girl said.

There was no handshake, and Simon decided to get down to business.

"May I speak to you alone, Miss Bannerman? It is important."

Mary Bannerman looked hesitantly at Peterson.

"Well, Jeff is . . ." she began, but Peterson interrupted her.

"If you're going to talk to him you might as well get it over with," he said, glancing at his watch. "I've got to get an early start in the morning."

"Fine," said the Saint. "Good night."

He had taken as instant a dislike to Peterson as Peterson had clearly taken to him, and he had very little desire to hide it. It was one of those moods that seemed best given free rein, especially since Mary Bannerman appeared to be completely enjoying the conflict.

"I'll see you, darling," she said to Peterson.

"Right," snapped the other. "Good night."

She closed the door behind him and turned to the Saint.

"Won't you have a seat, Mr Templar?" she asked. "Drink?"

"Neither, thank you," he answered. "I've come here a little late for a social call—as pleasant as that would be."

He preferred to stay on his feet for more reasons than one. If Mary Bannerman was in on the blackmail plot against Liskard, Simon wanted to be as mobile as possible in case of a sudden outbreak of hostilities. Standing, he could also get a more completely panoramic view of the room and the adjoining kitchen and sleeping sections—the latter of which consisted of an alcove separated from the main room by half-drawn gold curtains. On a rumpled double bed sat a teddy bear large enough to have frightened off a moderately muscled lion. The rest of the furniture was new and expensive. Most of the walnut shelf space was devoted to pop records, and the only reading matter seemed to be magazines with pictures of Mary Bannerman on the covers.

"I must say my heart's going pitapat," she said, perching on the edge of a chair. "If this isn't a social call, what is it?"

"I've just come from Thomas Liskard."

Mary Bannerman's face—which until then had worn a provocative smile that apparently was the big gun in her public relations arsenal—went blank for an instant, and then hardened into a scowl. She stood up abruptly.

"No friend of Tom Liskard's is a friend of mine."

"We're not friends, exactly," Simon said without the slightest ripple in his own calm.

"He sent you here?"

Simon was deliberately holding back to see if she would betray anything.

"In a way," he said noncommittally.

His cat-and-mouse game was having part of its intended effect, even if it was not producing any information. Mary Bannerman's eyes were bright with impatient anger.

"Why?" she demanded sharply.

"I think you know."

"I do *not* know! I haven't even seen that—that two-faced rat for years. So come to the point, won't you? Just hearing his name makes me want to fumigate the place."

Simon leaned casually back against one of the shelves of records.

"If you're so anxious to forget him, why did you keep his letters?"

Her angry face showed nothing new but a trace of puzzlement.

"How did you know anything about it in the first place . . . and in the second place, what business is it of yours *or* his?"

Simon's lips wore a faint and he was sure very irritating smile.

"I think the Prime Minister was bound to develop a certain interest in his old correspondence with you when he got a letter from somebody threatening to show the whole lot to his wife and the newspapers."

"That's a lie, or a bluff, or something . . ."

"Are you sure?"

"Of course I'm sure, because I still have the letters."

Simon gave her a slightly apologetic look as he answered, "That doesn't prove the threat was a lie or a bluff, I'm afraid."

She glared.

"I'll prove it, then. He can have them back—right now! Just a second . . ."

She whirled and went to one of the wall shelves and slammed a whole stack of records onto the sofa. She hesitated a moment, and then snatched down another armful of discs. A white envelope—small and unlike the one Liskard had received—fell to the floor, but there was no sign of any secret nest of *billets doux*.

Mary Bannerman turned to face the Saint with an entirely transformed expression.

"They're gone," she said.

"That did seem likely," Simon replied impassively.

He was leaning down to pick up the small envelope from the floor. It was heavy with metal. The girl took it from his hand and tossed it back on the shelf.

"Those are the keys to my wardrobes," she said. "Do you believe me, or should I . . ."

"What about the letters?" Simon interrupted.

The girl was no longer defiant and outraged, but stunned and frightened.

"I know you'll never believe me," she said, "but I don't have the slightest idea where they are. I put them down behind those records months ago when I first moved into this apartment. I remember seeing them there a few weeks back."

"I suppose any number of people could have taken them."

"But who'd want to? No one knew about them. I've never even discussed Tom with other people, even when I realized that he didn't love me and had just been using me. He's terribly selfish and ambitious, but I wouldn't do a thing like blackmail him. After all, I was . . . very fond of him."

Simon felt a growing sense of frustration. No amount of conversation with Mary Bannerman at the moment seemed likely to get him much nearer the truth.

"No theories, then?" he persisted.

"Wait a minute! Yes. I had a robbery here three weeks ago. They stole some jewelry and furs and cash. It never occurred to me that they might have taken the letters."

"Maybe they were after the letters, and the rest was a blind. Did the thieves get caught?"

"No."

"And you don't know of anybody who could have wanted to get the letters?"

"Not a soul."

"That covers the field of suspects pretty thoroughly. What are you doing for dinner tomorrow night?"

She was startled into truth.

"I . . . nothing," she said flatly.

"I'll pick you up at eight. Think this business over between now and then. Maybe you'll come up with some ideas. If not, we'll at least have fun."

He turned to the door. She watched him step into the hall, and even though he would not have bet a tin cufflink on her honesty, he felt a little sorry for her. She looked sadly distressed and preoccupied, just as a woman might be expected to look when a tormenting part of her past was brought suddenly to the surface of her thoughts.

"Mr Templar . . . I know I'm labelled a sinner . . . God knows what Tom has told you about me. But it doesn't follow that I am a pushover for Saints."

Simon smiled.

"Message received. We'll worry about these theological questions as they come up."

6

The next morning the Saint reported his progress—or lack of it—to Liskard by telephone.

"Is it true about the robbery?" Liskard asked when Simon had finished. "Do you think the letters were really stolen?"

"I'll have to check on it. I'll say one thing: either your friend is a first-rate actress or she's in the clear. But which it is I wouldn't care to guess yet."

"What about this man with her?" Liskard asked. "Who was that?"

"His name was Jeff Peterson," Simon answered. "Does that ring a bell?"

Liskard hesitated, then became suddenly excited.

"Yes. Very likely. Is he from Nagawiland?"

"Mary Bannerman did refer to him as a colonial."

"Then he must be the one. He's a sort of black sheep of a good family back there."

"You know him?" Simon asked.

"No. But I know his father. I sacked him from my cabinet six months ago."

Simon seemed to feel horizons expanding around him.

"That's a fascinating bit of news, to say the least. Why did you toss him out?"

"I'm allergic to alcoholics." His voice became momentarily acid. "I seem to attract them."

"And Jeff Peterson seems to attract Mary Bannerman."

Liskard was silent for an abnormally long time.

"How . . . is she?" he asked.

"She seems well enough."

"What is her attitude toward me?"

Simon, as much as he respected Liskard's political position, felt no particular sympathy for his self-inflicted romantic complications.

"I get the impression that she hates your guts and would gladly put a knife between your ribs if you came within range."

Liskard grunted.

"She's not the only one," he said half-humorously. "I think I'm the most popular man to hit England since the Luftwaffe."

"That's because you're a political realist," the Saint told him. "The world hates political realists. Everybody loves a liar if they love his lies. So buck up; the same fringe adores you, and you can always say you went down telling the truth."

"An optimistic thought."

"Well, you're not going down," Simon said. "Not if I can do anything about it. Time's short, though. I'll be in touch."

Not long after talking to the Prime Minister, who that afternoon would begin his negotiations with the British government, Simon drove over to Chelsea and checked on Mary Bannerman's theft story with the police there. Her tale was confirmed. The robbery had taken place one night about three weeks before, and several thousand pounds' worth of female frippery—mostly heavy metals and animal pelts—had been carted off to parts unknown. Not surprisingly, the police had made no progress toward apprehending the thieves.

The Saint had affairs of his own to attend to during the rest of the day which have nothing to do with this story. He got back to Upper Berkeley Mews at about four, as the cold winter evening already was descending on wet misty streets. With fond recollections of the sunny expanses of Africa, he settled down at a desk overlooking the mews to catch up on some bills which had accumulated while he was away.

Not long afterward he noticed, there below, plowing slowly along through the murk, a small gaily decorated van with pictures of ice cream cones and the words *Mister Snowball* inscribed on its side panels. Odd as it was, Simon devoted very little thought to that specimen of unseasonal traffic on his almost untraveled backwater until it passed again a quarter of an hour later going in the opposite direction. By the time it had come back again, and again, and then once more while he was dressing for dinner, he had developed a fairly complete theory as to its origin and contents. Its orbit was so regular that he decided to intercept it on its next passage.

He was about to step out his front door when his telephone rang. The Mister Snowball van crept by right on schedule, but Simon was forced to watch it from a window.

"Mr Templar," a man's muffled voice said through the earpiece of the phone. "I understand that Mr Liskard is anxious to recover certain letters."

"And where did you pick up that idea?" Simon asked coolly.

The caller was momentarily stymied.

"He'll need those letters if he doesn't want to be in very bad trouble. Go to Belfort Close. Park your car at the circle at the end. There is a gate into a small churchyard. You'll be met there."

"Sounds delightful," said the Saint. "Who brings the Maypole?"

"If Liskard wants the letters, you'd better be there . . . in an hour."

"Wouldn't it be simpler if you just dropped them by his headquarters? He might give you a reward."

"We'll discuss rewards when we see you."

"I don't suppose you'll tell me to whom I have the pleasure of speaking?"

"Be at Belfort Close in an hour."

If a click can be dramatic, the click at the other end of the line had a certain well-timed theatrical abruptness to it.

Simon hung up and went to a mirror and straightened his tie as he thought over the situation.

The amateurishness of his opponents was laughable. But it was also dangerous. The Saint was one of the most adaptable of men, but he was accustomed to fighting a sword with a sword, or a pistol with a pistol. The present opposition was placing him in the position of a fencer with a rapier encountering a wild-eyed peasant flailing the air with a pitchfork. He had to adjust his tactics to the non-professional mentality, which meant, among other things, adjusting to an enemy who was going to be stupidly logical as long as he thought things were going his way, but stupidly and unpredictably erratic as soon as he got confused.

It was also true that the opposition, however obvious they were about laying an ambush, were devilishly subtle about their motives. There still seemed to be no point at all to the whole affair except a desire to torment Thomas Liskard with worry. Even now, in the telephone call, there had been no demand for money. Most blackmailers preferred to get their loot as rapidly as possible and clear out before they could be trapped.

The Saint glanced at his watch. It was a quarter to seven. In a few minutes Mister Snowball would be cruising by again. Simon put on his raincoat, and slipped a small flashlight into his pocket. He stepped out onto the street just in time to see the ice cream van turn the corner, heading toward him. Then, as he appeared on the sidewalk it stopped several doors away and turned off its lights. If he had not been watching for it he might never have noticed it. The sky was totally dark now, and the street lamps were muted by a light fog.

He turned not toward his garage door, but toward the van. He walked up to it and looked in at the white-capped, white-jacketed driver.

"I'll have a pint of vanilla, please," he said politely.

The driver gulped and looked sturdily straight ahead.

"Closed," he muttered. "All out of everything."

The wide opening behind the driver, which gave him easy access to the interior of the van, was covered by a heavy curtain.

"Surely you must have something," Simon insisted, drawing closer. "A slab of tripe . . . or a fat cheese?"

"Nothing," said the driver.

But by then the Saint had put his hand on the door opposite the driver. He jerked it open and stepped quickly in to fling aside the hanging curtain. There like a great rosy-jowled toad squatted Chief Inspector Teal of Scotland Yard.

"Well, 'pon my soul, if it isn't ol' Mister Snowball himself!" cried the Saint. "As I live and breathe! Will wonders never cease? It's a small world."

"Would you at least shut the door?" growled Teal without moving.

"Gladly."

There was no passenger seat in the van. Simon stepped inside, closed the door, and moved through the curtains into the cargo area, where he took a seat on a carton facing Teal. The detective regarded him with a baleful eye and kept his hands stuffed deep inside his overcoat pockets.

"On closer inspection," Simon said cannily, "I believe you're not really Mister Snowball at all, but that old overweight operative, Claud Eustace Teal, *disguised* as Mister Snowball!"

"What are you up to, Templar?" Teal asked coldly.

"I might ask you the same, Claud," the Saint said reproachfully. Simon glanced around the frigid interior of the van, which in addition to Inspector Teal contained nothing more comfortably padded than a cardboard box. There was a two-way radio in one corner and a few notepads and maps in another. "It's not much, I suppose," Simon observed, "but I'm sure it's an improvement over what you used to do—at least from a moral point of view."

Chief Inspector Teal heaved a deep sigh and pulled a hand from his pocket. The hand contained a stick of chewing gum, which he proceeded to unwrap and fold into his mouth. "Are you through being funny?" he asked with exaggerated boredom.

"I'm not sure," said the Saint honestly.

"You've gotten mixed up with the Prime Minister of Nagawiland," Teal said.

"I've been to dinner with him, if that's what you mean," Simon admitted.

"And you went to the Chelsea Police Station today and asked a lot of questions."

"It was entirely a mission of mercy," the Saint said. "I took along a food parcel and said a few cheery words. It's the least one can do. Don't you . . ."

"You were asking questions about a burglary that was reported by Liskard's old girlfriend."

"She's hardly old," Simon inserted. "I doubt that she's a day over twenty-five."

"You won't get me off the subject," Teal said. "I know that Liskard got involved with this girl—romantically involved—when he was here before."

Simon leaned back and rested his shoulders comfortably against the side of the van.

"Nosey old goat, aren't you?"

"It's our job to know things about the men we're supposed to protect," Teal went on. "Apparently something funny is going on and you're involved in it."

"Just what do you think is funny?" Simon enquired.

"That's what I'm asking you," said Teal.

"All over England," said the Saint accusingly, "stately homes are being burgled, payrolls and bullion are being hijacked, safe deposits and bank vaults are being blown—and you want to sit here and swap funny stories. As a public-spirited citizen, I can't help you to goof off like this."

He started to get up.

"Wait," Teal said. "You've got no reason to keep vital information to yourself. And if you're thinking you can pull one of your tricks and get some money out of Liskard by teaming up against him with his old girlfriend, you're out of your head. Pull any of your Robin Hood stuff with an important man like that, and you'll . . ."

"Oh, I see, Claud," said the Saint. "I see it all. You've got it figured out, have you?"

"I have," Teal said proudly. "You may as well give up your little scheme right now."

Simon leaned forward and placed a long finger firmly against Teal's fat paunch.

"And you listen to me, old plum pudding," he said affectionately, prodding with the finger. "You're on the wrong track as usual. Yes, there is something going on, but no, I won't tell you what it is. Because if I did, you'd jump in with all your three flat left feet and bungle it. Let's just get this straight, though. We're both on the same side. I'm no more anxious for Liskard to get in trouble than you are, and if you'll lay off I may be able to keep him out of it. Lay off Mary Bannerman, too, unless you want to foul things up so badly that you'll be knocked back down to giving breathalyser tests to nursemaids pushing baby buggies in the park. Is that clear?"

The Saint's final emphasis with his finger was so forceful that Teal choked on his chewing gum.

"You haven't done anything yet," the detective said sullenly. "If you do, I'll be waiting."

"That will give you more sleepless nights than it will me," Simon told him. "And now, if you'll excuse me, I have a date."

He got out onto the cobblestones, and looked at the van and shook his head.

"I'm a little surprised," he said. "This seems so crude, even for you."

"You don't think we'd have it repainted just for your benefit, do you?" Teal said, with injured indignation.

"I guess you're right," Simon said. "An ice cream truck in winter would scare off any crook with a better brain than yours. But in these days of government economy, think how much you could save on prison maintenance by never catching anyone."

7

The Saint drove his car on an elusive route through side streets guaranteed to lose Mister Snowball, and then hurried on to Belfort Close, which was in the neighborhood of Maida Vale.

The short street, with the decrepit antiquity of its brick façades, was like a score of other streets in northwest London. Beyond the turning circle at the end of the cul-de-sac was a rusty iron fence with a gate sagging from the cumulative weight of generations of swinging children. The churchyard, an old one, was shadowed by trees and populated by a pygmy army of squat tombstones. Simon could see only dark outlines. The feeble lamps of Belfort Close behind him were made doubly ineffective by the misty night.

Someone with a rather unreal sense of melodrama had chosen the setting, if not the mists. The Saint, with his flashlight in hand, moved without particular stealth into the stoney darkness. If he had wanted to come on stage secretly he would not have chosen the entry planned for him by the telephone caller. But his object was not to surprise anybody, but to be surprised himself. Only in that way would he stand much chance of getting to the truth about Liskard's enemy.

"Come into my parlor, said the fly to the spider," he murmured to himself.

If he had tried to capture the blackmailer he might only have frightened him away. And if, as seemed more than likely, there was more than one person involved, the capturing of one might lead to the immediate release of Liskard's letters to the papers.

The lights of an automobile swung through the trees of the churchyard. Simon turned. A taxi was pulling into the circle at the end of Belfort Close and a man was getting out. The Saint could see only that he was tall and quite thin, even frail. The taxi left, and the man came into the churchyard. Simon aimed the flashlight at the stranger's face and turned it on when he was within twenty feet.

"Good evening," Simon said.

The man held a hand in front of his face until the light was switched off. Even so the Saint got a look at him, and he was unfamiliar.

"You're Simon Templar?" the man asked.

"What if I say I'm not?"

"I've come to talk business," said the thin man irritably. "Do you want me to leave?"

"Yes, but I'll have to put personal feelings aside for the moment. What's your deal?"

"Twenty-five thousand pounds for the return of certain letters," the man answered curtly.

"Very expensive," the Saint said mildly.

"It should be worth it to Liskard."

Most men would not have noticed the almost imperceptible change in the blackmailer's carriage. He was scarcely more than a silhouette, but Simon sensed the sudden rise in tension.

"Do you have any proof that you have the letters?" Simon asked.

He moved closer to the man, until he was within striking distance.

"I'll give you one," the blackmailer said.

He reached into his pocket and produced an envelope. The Saint moved to take it, and then suddenly shifted his weight and jabbed his flashlight straight into the man's ribs. In the same motion he whirled and confronted the man he knew would be just behind him. His eyes were accustomed to the darkness how, and he could see the second man's heavy-featured face and the wadded white cloth he was holding forward in one hand.

The Saint reached a quick decision. Obviously if there were two men involved, it was unlikely that the plot against Liskard was based on a simple desire for revenge on Mary Bannerman's part. Whether the demand for twenty-five thousand pounds had been genuine or a mere ruse to hold the Saint's attention, there was very possibly a wider membership in the scheme than had gathered together in the churchyard.

Simon decided—since his assailant was not about to use a knife or gun—to let himself be captured. He lunged at the thug behind him, took a glancing blow on his shoulder, and slipped to his knees. Immediately the thin man and his hefty friend pounced, and Simon held his breath and went quickly limp as the chloroformed cloth was pressed against his face.

"Easy," muttered the hefty one.

"These chaps live on their reputations," the thin one concurred. "Let's get him out to the car."

The Saint held his breath again as he was given a precautionary second dose of the anesthetic. Then the men picked up his apparently unconscious body and hurried with it to the side of the churchyard opposite Belfort Close. Simon could not open his eyes more than a crack, but he saw that he was being taken to a very ordinary black car parked on a deserted lane. His porters put him into the back seat, and the thin one sat next to him.

"Get rid of that rag," the thin one said.

"How long will it keep him under?" the other asked.

He tossed the cloth away and slipped into the driver's seat.

"Long enough," the thin one said. "If anybody asks, we just say he's drunk."

"Keep his head down until we're out of town."

The car jerked and moved away. Simon kept track of the turns, and presently recognized Harrow Road as they turned into and headed west in the bright lights and heavy traffic. Another amateurish move.

The thin man chuckled, looking at Simon slumped in the other corner.

"So much for the Saint. How to lose your halo in one easy lesson."

The hefty one gave a hoarse laugh.

"Right. Jeff's going to think it's too good to be true."

That name was all Simon needed and had been waiting for, but he had scarcely hoped to have his answer so soon.

"It is too good to be true," he said quietly.

The thin man jumped as if the door handle had suddenly spoken to him. The driver jerked his head around and almost swerved into the opposite line of traffic. Simon's right arm swept out and encircled the thin man's neck, locking it in a crushing hold.

"Stop!" the thin man croaked. "Do something!"

They were coming to a red light. The driver was groping in his jacket pocket, probably for a cosh. At the same time he was looking desperately for some way to turn into a side street, but he was hemmed in by cars piling up at the traffic signal. Simon simply gave the thin man's neck one last crack, which it would take a first-class osteopath to unstiffen, let him topple half conscious and gasping onto the floor, and stepped as casually out of the car as if he had been leaving a cab.

A policeman on the busy corner gave him a disapproving look as he strode across the inner line of traffic to the sidewalk and turned to wave goodbye to the driver.

"Sorry," Simon said sincerely to the policeman, "but with traffic the way it is these days it's almost quicker to walk."

Simon caught a taxi back to his car at Belfort Close. The time was seven-fifty. He could still make it to Mary Bannerman's apartment for his dinner date in less than a quarter of an hour.

As he drove, theories raced through his head. There was still no evidence that the girl was knowingly involved. Her boyfriend Jeff Peterson could easily have taken the Liskard letters without her knowing that he had the slightest interest in them. Maybe Peterson had engineered the robbery of her apartment in order to take her mind away from the possibility that the letters had had any special importance to the thieves. The motive could involve anything from politics to purely commercial considerations. Still, the oddity of the approach to Liskard, the somehow amateurish approach to monetary blackmail and the lack of demand for money or concessions of any other kind, left a great many questions still to be answered.

One was answered as Simon drove cautiously to the corner of Mary Bannerman's block. As he was about to turn, almost on the stroke of eight, she came out of the front door with Jeff Peterson, holding his arm, wearing a cocktail dress. Peterson wore a suit instead of the turtle-necked sweater in which Simon had seen him before.

"Going out to celebrate?" the Saint asked silently.

He pushed down the accelerator of his car and sped past the intersection. He circled the block and parked. Judging from their clothes, the happy couple were going to be amusing themselves rather than indulging in nefarious activities which would make them worth following. Simon thought he could learn much more by a visit to Mary Bannerman's apartment while she was out. He walked around to the building's front door and climbed the stairs to her flat.

As he made short work of her lock—whose type he had noted when he was there before—he thought over her role in the situation. The fact that she had been leaving with Peterson did not prove conclusively that she was in on the entire plot, but it seemed to rule out any presumption of her total innocence. If she had only decided to stand the Saint up, she would surely have left earlier, so as not to risk running into him as she was leaving and he was arriving. It seemed irrefutable that she had known for some time that Simon Templar was not going to be able to keep his date with her, and that she could safely and openly go out with Peterson without any chance of complications.

The lock submitted easily, and Simon stepped into the flat. A table lamp had been left on. The bed was still rumpled, the teddy bear still in place. The rooms smelled of the last sweet flurry of female departure: bubble bath, talcum powder, perfume.

The Saint put Venus out of his mind and tried to concentrate on Mars. The sooner he brought this little war in which he had become involved to a conclusion, the sooner he could be enjoying himself—if not with Mary Bannerman, with someone like her in all the ways that really counted.

He walked straight to the shelf on which the girl had claimed she had left Liskard's correspondence. There, where she had left it, was the white envelope which had fallen to the floor when Simon had visited her the previous evening. In it were keys, just as she had said, but one was not designed for her wardrobes or for any other domestic strong-hold. It was attached to a metal circle with "*Victoria* 571" stamped into it. Simon recognized it immediately as the key to a baggage locker at Victoria Station.

Before he left Mary Bannerman's flat he made a systematic search of her property and found that her teddy bear seemed to be stuffed with nothing more interesting than cotton, that she had a talent for eliciting torrid letters from men other than Thomas Liskard, and that she did, indeed, seem to be a bit short in the fur and jewel department for such a successful girl with so many rich friends.

Unfortunately, there was no evidence of any interest in Thomas Liskard on her part, or on that of her pen pals. The Saint was going to have to make another trip through the cold foggy night.

8

The trip to Victoria Station and back to Mary Bannerman's flat could have taken considerably less time if the Saint had not decided to have a peaceful dinner on the way. At Victoria he went directly to the baggage lockers—banks of large metal doors along one wall of a corridor—and found number 571. The key he had brought with him opened it, and there inside was one large brown leather suitcase. Without hesitation he took the bag, closed the locker, and walked like any busy and purposeful citizen out into the street.

He doubted that any of Mary's associates were keeping watch over the locker, but it was quite possible that one of Chief Inspector Teal's minions had been assigned to keep watch over the Saint. For that reason he took a devious course away from the station area, making quite certain that nobody was following him. Then he parked three blocks from the apartment house where Mary Bannerman lived, left his car, and walked the rest of the way carrying the suitcase. As he had anticipated, the door of her flat was still unlocked, as he had left it, and she had not come home. He went inside, latched the door behind him, and put the suitcase on the bed.

The bag was not locked. Simon flipped the catches and opened the lid. There in a thick wrapping of mink and silver fox was a modest Ali Baba's treasure of jeweled trinkets of all shapes and sizes. Whatever Mary Bannerman had done to deserve all that, she apparently had done very well. The Saint's experienced eye told him that the quality of the whole lot was quite high, and a closer inspection confirmed that all of it appeared to be her own. Her name was sewn onto the linings of the coats and her initials were engraved on much of the jewelry.

But much more interesting to Simon was the fact that what he had most hoped to find was not there. The suitcase contained only jewels and furs: there were no letters from Thomas Liskard.

Still, things were looking up. He had a lever and he had a place to apply its pressure—or would have, as soon as Mary Bannerman came home. Simon poured himself a glass of Benedictine from the well-stocked liquor cabinet, left the lights and furniture as they had been before he came, and went into the sleeping alcove and drew the concealing curtains tightly together. Then, with the suitcase opened beside him, and a selection of glossy magazines to pass the time, he propped himself up on the bed next to the teddy bear and sipped his Benedictine and waited.

About an hour later Mary Bannerman came home. To Simon's surprise, Jeff Peterson did not come in with her. There were no voices to be heard through the closed curtains, and only one set of footsteps. She moved about her living room humming dance music to herself, completely unsuspecting of the surprise that waited in her bed. She ran some water in the kitchen, then, unzipping the back of her black cocktail dress with one hand she threw open the curtains that hid her sleeping alcove with the other.

Her reaction to the tableau of Saint, suitcase, and teddy bear was worthy of a Mack Sennett classic. She froze, stopped unzipping, opened her mouth, and she seemed to have difficulty keeping her eyes in their sockets.

"Ho, ho, ho," said the Saint. "Won't you sit on Father Christmas's knee? He's brought you some lovely toys."

Mary Bannerman at first seemed more likely to collapse than to sit on anybody's knee, but the first shock wore off. She closed her mouth and removed a trembling hand from the zipper on her dress.

"Speechless?" Simon asked.

She tried not to see the suitcase of jewels and furs.

"What are you doing here?" she managed to say.

"Keeping our dinner date." He looked at his watch. "You're a little late. Three and a half hours, to be exact."

"I . . . couldn't make it."

Simon swung his legs off the bed and stood up. His tone became more brittle.

"You thought I couldn't make it, more likely."

She shook her head feebly. Then she seemed to pull her thoughts together a little and realized she had a right to take the offensive.

"What are you doing here?"

Simon waved a hand at the suitcase.

"I not only steal from the rich and give to the poor, I return stolen property to lovely young girls . . . in return for small favors, of course."

She could no longer keep herself from looking at the contents of the suitcase. Her brief spell of bravado was past. Her face looked frightened and young, and she seemed to be on the verge of tears. She sat on the edge of the bed as if her legs would no longer hold her up.

"What are you going to do?" she asked tremulously.

"First, I'll listen."

"To what?"

"To glamorous Mary Bannerman's true life story . . . of how she lost her baubles and found them again."

She sighed.

"All right. I ran into debt. I needed money, so I invented the robbery to collect insurance money."

"Reasonable enough. And then?"

"I couldn't keep the things here, of course, or tell anybody else, so I checked them at Victoria Station."

"What about Liskard's letters?"

"I don't know. When you asked for them, and I found them gone, I . . . kind of lost my head. I was afraid of what you might think—because of the blackmail you were talking about and everything—so I just said they'd been stolen, too. But I don't know. I thought they were there."

Simon let considerably more credence show on his face than he felt in his mind.

"Then you obviously had a real theft here which you didn't know about," he said. "Who could have taken those letters? More importantly, who would have wanted them?"

She got up and paced over to the record shelf and began pulling down all the records she had pulled down the evening before.

"Maybe they're here," she said a little feverishly. "I'll find them if . . ."

"They're not," Simon assured her. "I've already looked."

She turned back toward the bed and glared at him.

"You're a regular sneak, aren't you?" she snapped.

"No, I'm an extraordinary sneak. I see all and know all. So tell me—did Jeff Peterson take the letters?"

She looked indignant.

"Jeff? Of course not! Why on earth should he?"

"Maybe he's gotten himself into debt, too. Twenty-five thousand pounds is a nice amount of money for an hour or so of playing post office."

Mary Bannerman looked at him with puzzled anger and began to lose control of her temper.

"Twenty-five thousand pounds? I absolutely do not know what you are talking about, and I'm not interested to know. I happen to be in love with Jeff Peterson, and I'm not going to have you breaking into my apartment and insulting him. Go find the letters yourself, if you're so full of ideas. But whatever you do, just get out!"

Simon did not raise his voice.

"When and what did you tell Jeff Peterson about Liskard?"

The girl tightened her lips in rage, then shouted at him, "None of your damn business! Now get out before I . . ."

The Saint was smiling.

"Call the police?" he suggested. "Good. You can save me the trouble."

Her spirit crumpled again, and she looked hopelessly at the suitcase.

"You're not going to tell?" she asked. "Why?" She moved closer to him, and her voice was more pleading than angry. "Are you so perfect that you can't let anybody else get away with anything? What do you care about some old insurance company's money?"

The sweet scent of the room was concentrated in her clothes and hair and skin, and it was fairly obvious that she expected the effect of her proximity to be devastating.

"I don't care about the insurance company," Simon said. "What I care about is . . ."

She ran the tip of one of her fingers along his lapel.

"Wouldn't it be more fun to help me spend it than to take it away from me?" she murmured.

"Much more . . . as soon as you give me those letters."

She dropped her arms to her sides.

"I don't have them, I told you!"

"Then the moment of truth has arrived for you, darling."

Without turning his back on her, he began to repack the contents of the suitcase.

"What do you mean?" she asked,

"I mean you must find those letters and give them to me by ten o'clock tomorrow morning," said the Saint. "Otherwise I'll arrange a little *tête-à-tête* between you and the insurance people. And also with a friend of mine at Scotland Yard who's starving for a pinch."

She followed him to the door, ready to grab the suitcase, which he carefully kept just out of her reach.

"I've told you I don't have those letters!"

"If you don't, your boyfriend does. So get them . . . And if you release those letters to the papers I'll do worse than I've already promised." He stopped and looked at her just before he opened the door. "I'm just curious. If you're after money, why didn't you say so in the first place when you threatened Liskard? You might have gotten it instead of me."

"I'm not after *anything!*" she moaned. "I don't know anything!"

Simon stepped out into the hall.

"Then how is it you knew I was supposed to be fast asleep somewhere at eight o'clock this evening instead of picking you up here for dinner?"

It was a strictly rhetorical question, which was just as well, since Mary Bannerman was visibly incapable of answering it—at least in the brief interval before Simon closed the door between them and walked away down the hall swinging the suitcase and whistling to himself.

That was the last she saw of him for some time, but he saw her again very shortly. He almost ran to his car and then quickly drove it to a corner which gave him a view of the block where she lived. Within ten minutes her small sports car pulled out from the curb and headed for the Cromwell Road. Simon stayed within sight of her without making himself conspicuous in the moderate traffic. Within ten minutes they were on the M4 motorway heading west. When Mary Bannerman reached the Windsor exit she turned off and took minor winding roads for several more miles. Twice Simon turned off his lights briefly, so that she would be less likely to suspect that the same car was staying behind her on that unlikely route of twisting country lanes.

When the sports car turned off into one of the bordering fields in what could only be the direction of the river, Simon stopped his own car and got out. Along that part of its wandering course, about midway between its youth at Oxford and its maturity in London, the Thames flows quietly through small towns and woods and pastures. What buildings there are on its banks between the towns are private and well spaced, and there are many miles as rural and serene as they must have been at the time of William the Conqueror. Such stretches of the river's banks are popular with the owners of small cabin cruisers, who simply make fast a couple of lines to the shore and spend the night.

Apparently such a mobile and secluded hideaway was being used by Jeff Peterson and his friends who had entertained Simon in the graveyard. The fact that the Saint had heard the mention of a boat would have been of no particular immediate help if Mary Bannerman had not been thoughtful enough to lead him straight to its current moorings.

The red lights on the rear of her car had faded and disappeared into mists. Now Simon could no longer hear the sound of its engine. The only interruption of the silence was the lowing of a cow in the pasture through which she had driven. Then the cow was quiet again, and Simon moved through the gate and across the uneven soggy ground toward the river. The water was so close that he could smell it, and he decided it was wisest to stick close beside the fence which ran that way so as to be camouflaged by the trees which grew along it on the edge of the meadow.

He moved as quietly as his own shadow, and even so he disliked the degree to which he had to expose himself. If Peterson and his boys were the least bit clever, they would have a man posted to watch all approaches to the boat. So far they had not shown much sign of all that intelligence, but if they had begun to develop some efficiency the Saint might find himself in trouble.

Ordinarily he would never have approached the boat so directly. Ideally, he might have come up to it in another boat, or crossed over from the other side of the river. But he fully expected that Peterson's first move on hearing from Mary would be to take the boat to another spot on the river as a precautionary measure. The time Simon had in which to board the floating hideout—where he hoped to find not only the blackmailers but also Liskard's letters—might be limited to the next three or four minutes.

He went on as fast as he dared. He could see Mary Bannerman's small car, and a few feet beyond it, tied alongside the low bank, a grayish-looking, medium-sized cruiser with lights glowing behind the curtains of its portholes. There were no other cars. Apparently the boat had been moved there from another mooring up or down the river after its occupants had driven to it. Maybe the two from the church-yard were not there, although it seemed likely they should have hurried out to report their failure to Peterson.

There was not much to be gained by mere speculation. Between Simon and the boat, separating the pasture from the tow-path, was a ramshackle fence put together of wire and iron posts. The only inconspicuous way for him to get through was on his hands and knees. Holding his gun at ready, he dropped to the ground and started through an opening below the last strand of wire.

That was when a voice behind him said, "Stop there, Templar, or I'll blow your head off!"

9

There was no room for argument. The Saint was not in a position to move quickly or even to see behind him. His main emotion was sheer rage at himself. He had been in a thousand more dangerous situations, but rarely in one which he could blame so completely on his own carelessness.

"Just hold it there," the voice said. Then it rose to a shout. "Come on, Benson!"

The tall man from the churchyard appeared on the deck of the boat and jumped ashore.

"Drop the gun!" he ordered.

Simon obeyed, continued on through the fence, and stood up. Jeff Peterson came out of the trees carrying a rifle. The man called Benson picked up the Saint's pistol.

"Onto the boat," Peterson said. "Tie him up."

The hefty man from the churchyard came up from the boat's cabin, and Mary was with him.

"You're very observant," Simon called to her cheerfully. "I thought I'd kept out of sight most of the way."

"She didn't need to be observant," Peterson said. "Benson was watching the road."

Benson's rough-faced companion grabbed the Saint's arm and shoved him toward the boat. Simon yielded, and then with a sudden shift of balance pushed the man with a splash into the narrow space between the side of the boat and the short perpendicular drop of the bank. Amid the general consternation and cursing, Simon continued obediently—mindful of the two guns pointed at him—down into the cabin.

"Lie down on your face in the bunk," Peterson said.

Simon followed the order, and Benson tied his hands.

"Now I've got no clothes to put on and what am I going to do?" bellowed the man the Saint had shoved. "I'd like to bash . . ."

He was coming down the companionway, but the cabin, with a bunk on either side, was scarcely large enough for the four people who were already in it.

"Never mind, Rogers," Peterson interrupted. "Go pace around up top until you're dried out."

"It's foggy! It's freezing! What'll I do?"

"Try catching pneumonia," suggested the Saint.

The man lunged at him, but Peterson pushed him back.

"Let's keep our heads," Peterson said. "There's no point getting this far and then fouling things up."

"We don't need him!" Rogers said. "Let's drown the blasted nosey . . ."

Mary Bannerman broke in. Her voice was full of panic.

"What's the point?" she asked. "I mean, what's the point to any of this? Haven't we done enough?"

Simon rolled over on his side so that he could see the speakers without twisting his neck.

"Not as long as Liskard's still on his throne!" Peterson said.

"Or until your father is on it?" Simon asked.

Peterson turned on him.

"What do you know about my father?"

"Quite a lot. I think you could find a better cause than trying to avenge him. He may have been an able man, but he was sick."

"No sicker than Liskard's own wife," said Peterson.

"Liskard's wife isn't helping run a government," Simon said. "Even if your father got a rough deal, it's no reason to try to wreck your own country."

"Getting rid of Liskard would be a favor to my country," Peterson said.

"Amen," said Benson.

Simon nodded with new and somewhat sad understanding.

"I see. You people are the sturdy band of young patriots who are going to cast out the tyrant and make your country free, *et cetera, et cetera.*"

"Tom Liskard is a tyrant!" Mary said to the Saint.

"I don't agree," Simon answered. "I've been there, you know, and I've seen Nagawiland. Without Liskard, the place would fall apart . . . at least, right at this moment. I'm not saying he's indispensable forever."

"You're damned right he's not," Jeff Peterson put in. "The sooner we get rid of him the better it'll be."

Mary Bannerman looked at him with worried eyes.

"I wish you wouldn't put it that way," she said. "You promised me there wouldn't be any getting *rid* of anybody. I mean, discrediting Tom is one thing, and I agreed. That's why I gave you the letters. But . . ."

"If you think he's got dangerous ideas about Liskard," Simon said, "wait till you see what he does to me."

"What will you do, Jeff?" she asked.

"Let him go when we've finished."

Peterson did not sound very convincing.

"And what'll I do?" the Saint gibed. "Recommend you for a knighthood? If you let me go you'll get ten years in jail." He looked at the girl. "Don't you see where this is leading? If you're really just after revenge, haven't you had it? If you quit the whole thing now it won't be . . ."

Suddenly Peterson's hand lashed out and struck Simon's face so hard that he was knocked back against the wall of the boat.

"Jeff!" the girl screamed. "Stop it!"

"I'm going," Peterson said, avoiding the Saint's steady, burning eyes. "The letters will have gotten to Liskard's wife by now."

"You sent them?" Mary Bannerman asked in astonishment. "You said he'd have two days, and it's not . . ."

"That's not the point, is it?" Peterson asked crisply. "The point is to bring him down, and there's timing involved."

"What kind of timing?" the girl asked, puzzled.

The three men—Benson, Rogers, and Peterson—looked at one another. None of them answered Mary Bannerman's question.

"Keep her here," Peterson said, jerking his head toward her. "I want to be in town when this breaks. I'll take her car and I'll be at her flat. Even if anybody thinks I'm involved I should be safe enough there, and I'll be near a phone."

"Involved in *what*?" the girl asked desperately.

"Involved in the revolution," he said coldly.

She stared.

"*Revolution?* What . . ."

"Call it what you like," Peterson said. "You don't think we could bring down Liskard without replacing him, do you?"

"But that's no revolution. There are men who'll take over automatically . . ."

"And be no better than Liskard."

"If you turn this into a racial thing, Peterson—stirring up the people down there, playing on the Africans' grievances—you'll have another Congo blood bath."

Peterson was halfway up the companionway. He smiled.

"Well, as Lenin said, you can't make an omelet without breaking some eggs."

He disappeared onto the deck. Simon looked at Mary.

"We who are about to be cracked salute you."

"Jeff wouldn't!" she said foolishly.

Simon settled back on the bunk with weary resignation.

"Oh, I think he would. In fact, I think he will. If he's going to cause the deaths of several thousand people, what's one egg more or less? As a matter of fact, you're quite a dish yourself. Omelet?"

Mary turned to run up to the deck, calling out Peterson's name. Rogers, the most muscular of Peterson's fellow patriots, stopped her on the companionway.

"Sorry," he said. "Jeff wants you here."

"I don't care what he wants! He doesn't own me. I'm not his prisoner."

"Look again," Simon murmured.

The girl tried once more to shake off Rogers, who thoroughly enjoyed holding her. She yanked herself away and sat down furiously on the land-side bunk on the other side of the boat from Simon.

"What'll we do?" she said angrily.

Obviously she was not the type to fall apart under pressure, and she did not take kindly to being pushed around—both qualities being in Simon's favor.

"Why don't we try escaping?" he suggested.

Rogers laughed, but the thin man, Benson, took offense.

"Shut up!" he barked. "Both of you!"

Rogers chuckled again.

"Well, Bill, which of us guards these tigers and which stands watch out there in the fog?"

"Who'd come here now?" Benson asked.

"Never mind what you *think* might happen. One of us has got to keep posted where we can keep an eye on the road, and get Templar's car out of sight while we're at it."

Benson heaved a grudging sigh.

"All right, then. We'll toss for it."

They flipped a coin, and Rogers was chosen to stand first watch ashore. He took Simon's car key, put on a slicker, and left the boat

"Better keep on your toes, Benson," the Saint said.

Benson looked around uneasily.

"What are you talking about?"

"Miss Mary might bash you in the head when your back's turned."

"My back won't be turned," Benson said.

He sat down on the steps of the companionway facing into the cabin. At that point the Saint sat up and swung his legs, which were not tied, to the floor. Benson was alarmed and instantly on his own feet.

"Lie down," he ordered.

Simon stood up. Time was too short to allow for planning and caution. It was better to do something brash than nothing at all. He could only hope that Mary Bannerman would get the idea and go into action.

"Make me," said the Saint with a look of mystifying and total confidence.

The look threw Benson off balance. For anybody trapped in a tiny bit of space with his hands tied behind him to look confident was completely unnerving.

"I told you to lie back down," Benson said nervously.

"Going to call your mate to help?" Simon taunted him.

That did it. Benson's spidery frame marked him as a man without much physical strength, which increased his hesitation to get involved with a man of the Saint's reputation—even if his hands were tied—but at the same time made him all the more sensitive to aspersions on his courage. He moved toward the Saint, whose back was now to the door which led to the forward compartment of the boat.

"You asked for it, Templar," Benson said with forced toughness.

That was when Mary Bannerman picked up the heaviest thing she could lay hands on—a large metal Thermos jug—and slammed him on the back of the head. He fell to his knees without so much as a grunt, and Simon finished lulling him to sleep with a charitably restrained toe of his shoe.

"You're a bright girl, Mary. Now please untie me before that other creep decides to drop back in."

"I don't know," she said hesitantly. "You'll turn Jeff in, and . . ."

"Mary, do you realize what's going on? This scheme you got yourself involved in is no righteous crusade to force a bad leader out of office. It's a power play, and it means upsetting a very delicate equilibrium if it goes through. And when equilibrium is upset in a place like Nagawiland it means more than new elections. It means disemboweled women and men skinned alive . . ."

Mary flinched.

"I know," she said. "I've seen pictures."

"Well, you'll be seeing a lot more pictures like that if we don't manage to stop your friend Jeff. Liskard may be a rat in your book, and he may not be the best leader in the world, but he's a lot better than most."

Mary came to him and began tugging at the knots which held his wrists.

"I feel like a traitor," she said bitterly.

"If it makes you feel any better, Liskard never had any thought of using you—which I'm afraid is more than I can say for Jeff Peterson."

"Tom told you that?"

"Yes. Whatever he did, there was nothing coldblooded about it."

She stopped untying Simon's wrists.

"Still, I can't just . . . turn Jeff in like this. Isn't there some way we could stop him without having him . . . put in jail or anything like that? Especially since I might get put in jail, too, for helping him."

"We'll see," Simon said. "In the meantime . . ."

He had been testing the bonds which still held his arms together. Mary had loosened them enough that he was able, with a sudden twisting movement and some quick work with his fingers, to tear them away. As he did it, he spun to face her.

"In the meantime," he concluded, "you don't have to feel guilty. I got away all by myself."

She was frozen for a moment, and then she made a dive for the chart book, which she had dropped on one of the bunks. Simon knocked it aside and caught her squirming body up against his.

"See?" he said. "No guilt. You even fought back and tried to stop me."

"I could scream," she said tentatively.

She was squirming less. Simon smiled.

"Well, don't. We need one another. Try using your head for a change. Can you do anything except pose for pictures?"

"Such as what?"

"Such as cast off those lines while I get this scow's engine set to go. We'll drift out quietly, then turn on the power and take off full speed."

Mary did not offer any more arguments or resistance.

"I'll handle the engine," she said. "I've done it before."

They both went on deck as soon as Simon had used the rope that had been taken from his own wrists to tie up Benson. The fog was thickening, and he could scarcely see beyond the fence which ran along the shore, which conveniently meant that Rogers would not be able to see the boat either. Within a few seconds the Saint had cast off both lines and sent the boat drifting toward midstream with a shove of his foot against the bank. He joined Mary Bannerman at the wheel. The bow had been headed upstream. Now, as the current caught it, it began to turn downstream toward London and the sea. The shore was five feet away, then ten, but the boat had still not entered the main current in the center of the river. The eddies it formed near the shore began to move the boat back toward land.

"Start it," Simon whispered.

Mary Bannerman turned the ignition key. The engine turned over, coughed, and died.

"It's tricky," she said.

The boat had moved downstream only a few yards. It was turning and drifting back toward the bank. Mary tried the starter again. The engine seemed to catch, then stopped. In the abrupt silence Simon heard running footsteps on the murky shore.

"He's heard us," Mary said.

"Try it again before we run aground."

The Saint hurried to the stern, which seemed the part of the boat most likely to strike land first. The starter was grinding loudly. Rogers was yelling as he ran through the fog.

"Benson! What's happening? Is that you?"

Then suddenly he appeared among trees and mist on the bank as the engine at last grumbled into full rhythm. The propeller bit into the mud and then pushed free. The boat began to move back toward midstream. Rogers had already drawn his pistol, and he tossed off a wild shot in their general direction. The Saint ducked hastily behind the deckhouse.

"Get down!" he shouted to Mary Bannerman.

"Full speed ahead," she cried, "and damn the torpedoes!"

Rogers fired out of the fog three more times in rapid succession. One of his bullets smashed a pane of glass a few inches from the girl's head. She dropped to her knees, still holding the wheel. Simon heard her feeble exclamation.

"Oh, my . . ."

Rogers, who was just barely visible, started to run down the riverside parallel to the boat, but with the help of the current they were moving much faster than he could, and then he slipped and tripped over something and went sprawling.

"That's one torpedo we won't have to worry about any more for the present," Simon said.

"He . . . he really was shooting at us," Mary stammered shakily.

She got to her feet and Simon steadied her with an arm around her shoulders as he took the wheel.

"That's revolution," he said. "Remember, you can't make an omelet without . . ."

"I know, I know," Mary said.

Simon squinted into the misty dark.

"There's just one thing. I wish you transformers of society had picked a more suitable time of year for your egg cracking. Like Easter, for instance."

"What'll we do now?"

"Get to a telephone, and then back to London as fast as possible."

"In *this?*"

"No. We should be able to get a cab in Windsor even at this hour. In the meantime, tell me everything *you* know about this plot against Liskard."

"You know it," she said. "Jeff got the letters from me. We were going to send them to the papers and force Tom to resign."

"Why all the pussyfooting around? Why didn't you just publicize the letters right away without tipping Liskard off?"

Mary frowned and shook her head. Simon was piloting the boat, and she was standing close to him, hugging herself to keep warm.

"It seemed unnecessary to me. A bit extra sadistic. It was Jeff who insisted on it. I thought it would be safer and better all around if we just got it over with as fast as possible."

"That would have been the reasonable way," the Saint agreed. "So unless your boyfriend's unreasonable he must have had something else in mind."

"Don't call him *my* boyfriend," Mary said bitterly. "And what else could he have had in mind?"

"Something much worse than you did."

"What?"

"We'll find out soon enough," Simon said grimly. "I see lights up ahead."

10

The cluster of lights the Saint had seen through the fog marked the site of a cottage on the right bank of the river. There was a sound of loud dance music even above the rumble of the boat's engine.

"Maybe we can get a lift into London from there," Simon said to Mary Bannerman.

Then came a muffled shout from below.

"Hallo! Who's there?"

"I'll have to take care of our patriot," Simon said. "Cut the engine down and make a circle or something before we dock."

He hurried below to the cabin, where Benson lay trussed on the floor. He stopped shouting and stared with open fear at the Saint.

"What are you going to do to me?" he whimpered. "Where are we?"

"You don't happen to have any more chloroform among your stores, do you?" Simon asked him. "You used to be rather partial to it, I remember."

Benson could only gape as Simon pulled out a knife and then did not use it on the thin man's scrawny neck but on one of the bunk sheets.

"Open wide and take your medicine," Simon said to him.

"What do you mean?" Benson quavered.

"Open your mouth," Simon repeated harshly.

Benson opened, and the Saint shoved a generous wad of cloth into his mouth, then wrapped a long strip of the sheet around his head several times to cover his mouth.

"Now try to yell," Simon said.

"Mmp!" grunted Benson unhappily.

The Saint tore a flyleaf out of a book from one of the shelves and wrote a brief message on it: "I am a bad man. Please hand me over to the police."

He folded the note and tucked it into Benson's shirt so that most of the paper would be plainly visible to anybody entering the cabin.

"I hope nobody will come and find you before Claud Eustace Teal can send somebody out to pick you up, but I can't take you with me and I'm afraid Miss Mary wouldn't approve of my throwing you overboard. You can wait for your pals in jail. Nighty-night."

Simon left the cabin in darkness and rejoined Mary Bannerman at the helm.

"Now," he said, "let's bring her in."

He steered the cruiser to the landing stage and skillfully brought her to rest without the slightest bump. Before the current could start to affect the craft he cut the power and made fast to shore. Three men—two with drinks in their hands—were already coming out of the cottage toward the river to see what was happening.

"Stay here, Mary, and just follow my lead," he told her, and went to meet them.

"Come to join the party?" one of the men asked.

They were young, well-dressed, and obviously well along in the process of enjoying themselves. A girl came to the door of the cottage and looked out, sipping from a tall glass.

"We're not party-crashing," Simon said. "I'm afraid we have a bit of an emergency. My wife is ill and I must get her to our doctor in London. Could I use your phone to call a taxi?"

"Oh, the poor thing," said the girl in the doorway. "We can't let her just . . . pop off or something."

"None of us here going to London," mumbled one of the young men drunkenly.

"Would twenty pounds make the trip worth your trouble?" Simon asked.

The tipsy one who had spoken just before the girl was the first to answer.

"It jus' happens I have to go London! It jus' happens!"

"You're not going anywhere," one of his soberer companions said. Then he spoke to Simon. "Of course we'll help. I'm the only one fit to drive. Is she really bad—your wife, I mean?"

"Not terribly, yet," Simon answered. "It's a sort of attack she gets sometimes, and only her own doctor knows what to do about it."

He went back to get Mary, who made a face at him as he helped her out of the boat. She sagged against him as he walked with her toward the cottage.

"Now's your chance to do some more acting," he said under his breath. "Just moan in a spartan sort of way occasionally and don't say anything. If anybody asks you questions just shake your head and close your eyes."

The sober young man came to help.

"Shall we get right to the car or would she like to rest here first?" he asked.

"It's best to go straight to town," Simon answered. "If you have a telephone I'd like to make a call, though."

"Go right ahead. It's in the bedroom on the left. I'll help your wife into the car."

Simon made his way through the front door of the cottage and the girl who had come out to see him showed him to the telephone. He dialed Scotland Yard as soon as he was alone behind the closed door.

"Hullo," he said when he received an answer. "This is Simon Templar . . . Yes . . . Exactly. I have a message for Inspector Teal . . . Yes . . . There's a man named Jeff Peterson he'll want to take into custody immediately because he's a threat to the Prime Minister of Nagawiland—Prime Minister Liskard. Do you have that clear?"

The functionary at the other end of the line had it clearly enough, but he was skeptical.

"Just get the message to Teal and make sure he knows who sent it," said the Saint. "Peterson should be at the flat of a Mary Bannerman in Chelsea. You can get her address from the directory. It's very urgent. Secondly, I've another present for him out here—wait just a minute."

He put down the phone and went to the door of the bedroom.

"Where are we, please?" he asked the girl in the adjoining living room.

"Forty-eight Meadow Road."

Simon went back to the phone and gave the address.

"It's somewhere between Bray and Windsor on the south bank of the Thames," he said. "If you'll have some men sent out you'll find one of Peterson's cronies tied up in the cabin of a boat just in front of the cottage."

"And how did all this happen?" the Scotland Yard man asked.

"I don't have time to talk now. I'll tell Teal later."

He left the phone and hurried out to the car.

"I'll sit in back and let her stretch out with her head in my lap," Simon said. "And if you don't mind it would be best if we don't talk. Here's your twenty pounds."

The young man protested, but took the money. Then, as Simon cradled Mary's head and comforted her, the driver pulled his sports sedan into the road and aimed it toward London.

Less than an hour later they pulled up to the entrance of Nagawi House. The pickets had exhausted their zeal and gone home; the gate was closed, and a lone uniformed guard spoke through its bars when Simon got out of the car.

"Have you any sort of official pass?" he asked.

"We're coming to the party," Simon said.

The driver of the car, meanwhile, gaped as Mary Bannerman sat up, blinked her eyes brightly, and stepped out onto the sidewalk next to the Saint.

"The party's over long since," the guard said.

"As a matter of fact it's urgent business," Simon told him. "The Prime Minister knows me. I have information he'll want immediately."

"Have you telephoned for an appointment?" the guard asked.

Mary Bannerman began quietly explaining some of the true situation to the driver of the car.

"I have a very particular reason for not telephoning," Simon said. "And I'm sure Prime Minister Liskard doesn't make appointments in the middle of the night."

"I know he doesn't. You'd best come back tomorrow."

"I'm telling you it's urgent," Simon said angrily. "The Prime Minister's life literally may depend on it."

Only then did the guard look particularly interested.

"I'll call his secretary, then," he said.

"No," Simon insisted.

"Why not? I'll do it now."

Simon looked desperately toward the lighted windows on the ground floor of the big house. Behind him the driver of the car was saying a puzzled good night. He turned his car back in the direction from which he had come and drove away.

The sound of a shot cracked out through the night from one of the rooms of Nagawi House. The guard stiffened and then started running toward the front door. Lights flashed on inside the house. Simon grabbed Mary's hand and hurried with her around the corner of the wall away from the gate.

"Where are we going?" she gasped. "They haven't shot Tom, have they?"

"I'm going over the wall, and you should know whether they've shot Tom or not."

"I don't know! It was just . . ."

"I believe you. Listen. Get away from here. Catch a taxi and check in at the Hilton—you can say you missed your last train home, since you've got no luggage. Stay in your room until I contact you. All right?"

"All right."

"Good girl. Now, if you'll excuse me . . ."

They were next to the wall at its nearest distance to the house, in a sort of alleyway between it and the next building. Simon stepped back, and then with a light leap he caught the top of the wall and swung his body up and over it.

On the inside, he set off at a run toward the rear of the house. That area was lighted only by a single diffuse floodlight, and no one seemed to be keeping watch. With the night guard to testify that he had been at the front gate when the shot was fired, he had no fear of being accused of having anything to do with that, and now he only wanted to get to the scene of the shooting as fast as possible. He remembered the location of the Prime Minister's study, which was near a corner of the building opposite the side on which he had entered the grounds.

When he reached the study windows he heard excited voices inside. One of the windows was open, its curtains stirring in the cold night air. Simon, in the light which came from the room, looked at the wet, soft earth along the side of the house. The only footprints were his own.

He hoisted himself up on the windowsill and vaulted into the study.

The effect on the people already there was dramatic in the extreme. Anne Liskard, who was in her nightgown, screamed. A half-dressed manservant fell back against the entrance door. Todd and Stewart, in pajamas and dressing gowns, froze and gaped. Another man, in a suit, had his hand on the telephone.

The only member of the tableau who did not react was Thomas Liskard. He was seated in his large chair with his head on the desk. In one of his hands was a pistol. Blood covered one side of his head and stained the blotter where it lay.

"What are you doing here?" Stewart demanded of the Saint in a shocked voice.

"I was at the gate when I heard the shot, so I got here as soon as I could—over the wall and around the house. I thought I might catch somebody trying to run away."

"You'll have some explaining to do yourself," Todd said. "But he shot himself. There was nobody to run away."

Anne Liskard had been sobbing as Simon entered, but now she broke in frantically. "Why doesn't somebody do something?"

"We can't do much, really," Todd replied in a lower voice. "He's dead."

Simon was bending over Liskard. Below the hand which held the gun was a scrawled note:

There's no other way for me.

The Saint touched Liskard's wrist. The man who was dressed, who turned out to be the secretary, was dialing a number on the telephone.

"Get away from him," Stewart snapped, coming toward the Saint.

Simon straightened up and addressed the secretary.

"Who are you calling?"

"The police, of course."

"Make it an ambulance," said the Saint. "The Prime Minister is still alive."

11

The Saint's words had almost as electric an effect as his entrance into the study had had. Anne Liskard gave a sharp cry and ran to her husband. The men stared.

"Better not touch him," Simon said. "The sooner a doctor gets to him the better."

The secretary called for an ambulance, and set about herding out the lesser members of the staff.

"Are you sure?" asked Todd, the Foreign Minister. "He doesn't seem to be breathing."

"Try his pulse," Simon said.

The others, satisfied that Liskard was alive, broke into a babble of conversation.

"Call Chief Inspector Teal of Scotland Yard," Simon said to the secretary. "He knows I've been working with Liskard on a problem of his. He'll want to know about this, I'm sure. I'm surprised you haven't heard from him already this evening."

"We have," the secretary said. "I took a call from him to Mr Liskard about twenty minutes ago. I'm to monitor calls, you know, and take notes. It seems the police had just picked up a man named Peterson, who was suspected of being in on some scheme about the Prime Minister."

"Who else knew about the call?" Simon asked.

"Todd and I were saying good night to him in his room when the call was put through," Stewart said. "But really—you're taking a lot on yourself, questioning us as if we were . . ."

"The Prime Minister asked me yesterday evening to help him," Simon replied. "He'll confirm that if he's able."

"But why would he do this?" Stewart wanted to know.

"It's my fault!" Anne Liskard blurted suddenly. "He and I had a scene tonight, when we were alone, and I wouldn't listen to any explanations from him, or forgive him. I . . ."

"He'd hardly kill himself over a family quarrel," Stewart said gently.

"It was more than that," the woman said. "You'll all know anyway. The newspapers know. There were letters . . . from Tom to . . . another woman." Her voice broke, and then she went on. "Somebody sent some of them to me, with a note saying others were going to the newspapers. Tom asked me to keep it quiet, but I . . . I lost my temper, of course. I told him this was the end of his career."

She began to cry, and sank down into a chair. The secretary, meanwhile, had completed his call to Scotland Yard. He went to the hall to speak to members of the delegation and staff who were being kept from the study by some senior member of the group.

"In any case," Todd said heavily, "it does seem to be the end of his career." He picked up a stack of papers near Liskard's elbow. "These apparently are photostats of the letters. Just the first one's enough to . . ."

He broke off, with a glance at the Prime Minister's wife.

"But the papers would think twice about printing that kind of thing, unless they had absolute proof that it wasn't forged," Simon said.

"And I don't mind saying this next in front of Mrs Liskard, since it ought to make her feel better. When you think of it, honestly, what sort of shocking news is it when a man, even a man in politics, got himself involved in a personal entanglement of this kind?"

"It could ruin him politically," Todd insisted. "Especially at this point."

"I've heard those sorts of rumors about almost every head of state in the world," Simon said, "and I'm sure I'm not the only citizen who hears them. Something like this actually might be good for a man in Liskard's place. People are more sympathetic with the victim of a blackmail plot than they are disgusted with a man who shows some manly weaknesses."

A siren was approaching, growing louder along the street in front of Nagawi House.

"Well what exactly is your point?" Stewart asked.

"That we keep all this quiet—about the letters?" Todd speculated dubiously.

"I'm suggesting that there's much more to this supposed blackmail plot than we seem to be assuming," the Saint answered. "It never made a lot of sense anyway. Now it's coming clearer what's really going on."

"What?" Stewart asked.

A still partially unbuttoned butler let himself back into the room.

"The ambulance is here. They're on their way in."

The next ten minutes were taken up with the removal of Liskard on a stretcher to the ambulance. At the end of that time, as the ambulance was pulling out of the drive, its blue light spinning above the driver's compartment, a police car with a similar spinning light pulled in the other side. Simon, who was standing on the steps of the house with the others, watched expectantly as the rotund form of Chief Inspector Teal evacuated itself from the car and puffed heavily up to the group. As he was about to speak, Teal's eyes fell on the Saint and his preparatory air of self-importance collapsed to a semblance of mere controlled dignity.

"I'm sorry to hear about this," he said to Liskard's countrymen in general. "Where did it happen?"

They led the way through the house, and Teal spoke to Simon.

"I got your message, and we found Peterson at Mary Bannerman's apartment. But now it looks as if he wasn't any threat at all—and you're going to have a lot to explain." Teal's pink face grew almost tomato colored as he strode along the hallway. "While we were wasting our time there . . ."

"Somebody else shot Liskard," Simon supplied. "But Peterson is in on it. You weren't wasting your time—for once."

Teal faced him at the study door.

"Shot Liskard? He shot himself, didn't he?"

"No," Simon said. "He wasn't the type. Much too levelheaded to be thrown this far by a lot of old love letters. And besides, he has a sense of duty. He wouldn't just bow out and let his country fall into chaos."

"This way," Todd said.

Teal went into the study, received a complete rundown on events, and looked over the evidence. When he had examined the gun, the blotter, the furniture, the suicide note, and the photostats, he pondered the situation as he stood in the center of the room with his thumbs hooked in the belt of his capacious dark blue coat.

"Pity he was moved," he grumbled. "If there's any doubt about the question of suicide . . ."

"That's true," Simon said thoughtfully. "We could have let him bleed to death so as to keep the evidence tidy."

"What do you mean, doubt?" Anne Liskard asked.

She had regained control of herself and was showing more poise and energy than Simon had seen in her since their first meeting.

"Mr Templar here seems to believe your husband may have been shot," Teal said.

Simon nodded. Teal's assistants, Stewart, and Anne Liskard looked toward the desk as he spoke.

"If you'd seen the way he was lying, even you would have noticed it yourself, Claud. It was an amateurish job, done in a hurry. If you're going to kill yourself you don't go through the discomfort of twisting your arm around and shooting yourself from some odd angle behind the ear."

"You might," Teal said, instinctively rejecting anything the Saint proposed.

"*You* might," Simon said to him, "but Liskard was never an idiot."

Teal walked stolidly to the window.

"And there's this," he continued. "Was this window open when you found him? It's a cold night. He wouldn't have left it open, would he?"

"Not likely," Stewart said. "In fact he was very sensitive to cold. Most of us are, raised in a tropical climate."

"So," said Teal, "someone may have come in, shot him, left the note, and escaped through the window."

"Great Scot!" the Saint exclaimed admiringly. "I think he's got it!"

The detective looked at Simon with the face of a soured persimmon.

"Is there any reason for Mr Templar to be here?" he enquired stiffly.

"He and my husband were working to catch these blackmailers," Anne Liskard explained. "Mr Stewart and Mr Todd will tell you the rest. I must get dressed and go to the hospital. There may be something I can do for Tom."

She went toward the door as Todd came back from the hall.

"I've phoned our PRO," he said to the group in general. "He'll do what he can to squelch any stories in the papers about the letters."

Simon turned to Teal after Anne Liskard had gone on before him into the hall.

"Could I speak to you alone for a minute, Claud?"

Teal followed him out to the driveway where they could speak without being overheard. Simon filled the detective in on what had taken place since they had met in the Mister Snowball van.

"Now listen, Claud," he said firmly. "I know you'd like to devote yourself exclusively to proving me wrong, but there's more at stake than your reputation and my self-interest."

He lowered his voice. "You won't find any footprints outside the window except mine, and the guard on the gate himself can testify that I was outside these grounds when the shot was fired."

"So it *was* a suicide attempt?"

"No. It was attempted murder. By somebody in the building."

"Who?" Teal retorted.

"I may be brilliant, but I'm not totally omniscient. It was undoubtedly somebody in on the plot with Jeff Peterson. I'm sure the scheme was something like this: use the letters to give Liskard a motive for suicide, and then commit the suicide for him since he wouldn't do it himself—leaving the window open as a false clue to murder if the suicide setup wasn't convincing enough. His death was to be the cue for a revolution of some sort in Nagawiland, probably in the name of equality and democracy, but in fact a power grab. Peterson and his father, who's back in Nagawiland, were in on it, but Peterson's father would never be accepted as head of state. He's a notorious alcoholic down there. The top man still hasn't blown his horn."

"So you have it all figured out," Teal said slowly. "Except the small matter of who did it."

The Saint shrugged.

"I can't do all your work for you, Claud—I'm only trying to do most of your thinking. Now if you'll try to control your natural envy of superior intellects, I'll let you in on a brilliant plan I've come up with for catching the leader of this conspiracy."

Teal managed a rather theatrical sneer.

"What plan would that be?" he grumbled. "Torture the ones we've caught until they tell who the boss is?"

"No, Claud, I'm suggesting we *not* use standard police methods this time." Simon looked warily around. "If you want to catch your man before breakfast, don't waste any more of my time here—and don't try to keep me out of that hospital. Whatever other ideas you have about me, you know me well enough by now to know that murdering a man like Liskard isn't my kind of fun. But if you'll cooperate with me this time, you can have all the glory."

His tone was no longer mocking, and the detective had jousted with him for long years enough to recognize his sincerity.

Teal peered at him torpidly, chomping his gum like a shrewd and very thoughtful cow. A cartoonist depicting the scene might have drawn a small and almost wattless bulb glowing feebly above his head.

"You're thinking of a trap," he stated expressionlessly.

"Good for you, Claud, old tortoise," Simon congratulated him. "And it needs you to help rig the cheese."

12

Nearly three hours later, on the third floor of the Edgington Hospital, a doctor appeared at one end of a corridor as two other doctors came out of a room and walked away along the corridor in the other direction. Another door on the same corridor was flanked by a uniformed policeman and a plain-clothes detective. A student nurse carrying a covered metal tray came out of that room and followed the two doctors.

No one paid any particular attention to the doctor who then walked alone down the corridor. He wore a white smock which covered his body from his shoulders to his knees. Over his mouth and nose was a white mask, and a white cap closely covered the top of his head and his forehead. At the guarded door he merely nodded to the detective, opened the door, and stepped in. Beyond a small alcove was the patient's bed. The patient lay still, his own head thoroughly bandaged. Only his eyes were not covered by gauze, and they were closed.

A nurse who was sitting near the bed stood up and looked at the doctor in surprise.

"I thought he was supposed to sleep," she said.

"He is," the doctor whispered. "But his reaction in the next hour may be critical. Please get everything prepared for a transfusion if necessary. And while you're at it, you'd better also ask for an oxygen tent."

The nurse peered at his eyes.

"I'm sorry, doctor, but I don't recognize . . ."

"Bronson," he said impatiently. "I'm on the Prime Minister's personal staff—from Nagawiland. Now, if you please . . ."

The nurse, accustomed to obeying doctors without question, thinned her lips, nodded, and left the room.

Instantly the doctor hurried to the bed. The patient lay still, his breathing slow and shallow, only his closed eyes showing through the bands of gauze and adhesive that swathed his head. With a swift glance over his shoulder at the door, the doctor pulled something that looked like a thin pointed stick from beneath his white smock. He bent over the bed, bringing the long slender shaft down toward the throat of the man in the bed.

The patient suddenly came to life. He rolled violently toward the doctor, catching him low in the stomach with a foot that shot out from between the sheets and sent him tumbling back across the room. The doctor's eyes were wide with surprise and panic. The patient flung back the covers and sprang out on his feet. The doctor reeled back toward the door, wildly swinging the stick to cover his retreat, but the patient now had an automatic in his hand, pointing accurately at the center of the doctor's chest

"If I were in the movies," came Simon Templar's voice from behind the patient's mask, "I'd say, Sorry to interrupt your operation, doctor, but this time I'm afraid you're the one who gets stuck."

The doctor froze, his back to the alcove which led into the main corridor.

"Now drop that magic wand—which looks to me like a souvenir Nagawi arrow, probably dipped in some jolly native poison," Simon said, pulling off his own bandages.

The other man seemed about to obey, but then he drew back his arm and flicked his wrist, and the arrow flashed through the air toward the Saint. Simon ducked aside, and the sharp stained point whipped past his ear and clattered against the wall beyond the bed in which he had been lying.

He could easily have shot his opponent dead in that single second, even while he was dodging the arrow, which might actually have been what the other was hoping for, if his last desperate throw failed to inflict a scratch which could likely have been lethal. But the Saint wanted him alive. So when the man followed the arrow with a wild suicidal lunge at him, Simon once more held his fire, but sidestepped and deflected the blow with a numbing karate cut into the forearm. His own right hand jabbed the gun muzzle cruelly into the "doctor's" belly. His left caught him flat on the side of his head, and then snatched away the white mask.

"Foreign Minister Todd," Simon said pleasantly. "I suppose this is a sample of how your followers would have gone back to nature if your little revolution had come off?"

Todd tried another futile swing even though he was dazed and against the wall. He succeeded only in knocking over a table lamp. Simon swung him around and locked him in a comparatively painless if undignified judo hold.

"One thing you're not," the Saint said regretfully, "and that's a fighter. I suppose those diplomatic cocktail parties aren't the best exercise in the world. All right, everybody—the show's over."

The door of the communicating lavatory burst open, and half a dozen people came through it in fairly rapid succession. Among them were two police officers and Chief Inspector Claud Eustace Teal.

Simon released Todd with a motion that swung him directly into Teal's arms.

"Liskard's dead?" Todd asked as he was put in handcuffs.

"Don't sound so hopeful," Simon answered. "You're as bad a shot as you are a brawler. You fractured his jaw, but that should only increase any politician's popularity."

Anne Liskard had also come into the room. She stared at Todd with shock and horror.

"Why?" was all she could say.

"He's a tyrant!" Todd screamed hysterically.

"And you wanted to take his place—which is both more truthful and to the point," Simon put in. "Obviously you didn't have any hope of getting all the way to the top on your own merits, so you thought it easily might be worth a couple of thousand lives to get there through a coup."

"It's a revolution!" Todd raved defiantly. "It can go on without me."

"There is no revolution," Anne Liskard said to him icily. "And I don't know how even somebody as low as you could have the nerve to use that word for the bloody little game you're playing."

She and Todd glared at one another. Teal took the prisoner's arm and pulled him toward the door.

"Coming, Templar?" he asked.

"No, thanks, Claud. I'll let you bask in whatever limelight you can scrape together at this hour of the morning. The one thing I want in the world at this point is some sleep."

Teal and his troops left with Todd. As Simon followed, Anne Liskard touched his arm. Her whole manner had changed since he had first met her.

"I don't know what I can do to . . ."

"Thank me?" the Saint said. "Just one thing. Try to get the past in perspective, and be nice to your husband. Until anyone better comes along, Nagawiland really needs him. He's a good man."

She looked at him seriously, and then her tired face softened into a smile.

"I'm way ahead of you on that," she said. "I've already made enough good resolutions to last me through a dozen New Years."

Simon looked back over his shoulder as he walked away.

"And take care of yourself," he said. "That's a worthy cause, too."

At ten in the morning of the same day the Saint settled down beside the telephone in his own home in Upper Berkeley Mews. It had begun to snow lightly, and his own personal view of London was beginning to look like sugared cake. The fog was already gone, and by nightfall the stars would probably be as sharp as crystals in a clear sky.

And there would be no Mr Snowball truck lurking in a gray street. Mr Snowball would be happily taking credit for his latest victory over evil, and the gray street would no longer be gray but pure and sparkling white in the pale sunlight.

"Good morning—London Hilton," came the response to his dialing.

"Miss Bannerman, please," Simon said.

A little later Mary Bannerman answered.

"Did you think I'd forgotten you?" Simon asked.

"Oh, thank goodness it's you!" she exclaimed. "Are you all right? I've heard everything on the radio—about Jeff and the others being arrested, and Todd, and . . . and you were right. They were planning to take over in Nagawiland."

"In fact, their buddies down there murdered two good men before word got there that Liskard was still alive—contrary to their expectations. But it could have been much worse. If the tribes had gone on a rampage . . ."

"I can imagine," she said. "And Tom . . . how is he?"

"He'll be all right. Todd must have panicked when he got word that Peterson had been picked up, and his hands were shaking when he tried to fake a Liskard suicide by himself. Then he had to make one last mad try at the hospital—but he blew that, too."

"I'm glad." The girl's voice was subdued. "Tom'll be able to carry on, then?"

"Yes. In fact this could make him a hero. And his wife shows signs of being something more than an anchor, for the first time in years."

Mary was silent for some moments before she spoke again.

"I suppose the police will be around to get me soon."

Simon deliberated.

"I've thought it over," he said. "Until now I've never gone in much for psychologists' theories about the treatment of criminals, but I'll give even a bad idea a chance. You can consider yourself under suspended sentence. I'm taking personal responsibility for your rehabilitation. You'll have to own up to your little insurance swindle, of course, but if you give the money back I'm sure the Company won't prosecute you."

"But Jeff will tell . . ."

"Tell what? That you gave him those letters? They were yours to do what you liked with—except use for blackmail. But nobody was ever asked for money, except me. And that was only a pretext for something else, so I've decided to forget it. You weren't involved in any of the real violence.

"Which seems to leave you in the clear. Aside from the usual requirement of keeping in close touch with your probation officer."

"Oh, Simon!" she said with incredulous relief shaking in her voice. "Tell me when . . ."

PUBLICATION

HISTORY

The stories in this book started life as episodes of *The Saint*, starring Roger Moore; "The Persistent Patriots" first aired on Friday, 6 January 1967, whilst "The Art Collectors" first aired the following week. Charteris liked the script for "The Persistent Patriots," which was originally called "Recoil," noting that, "the script of 'Recoil' is first-class, and the weaknesses I pointed out in the synopsis have been well taken care of. Although I still feel that most experienced mystery-watchers will automatically suspect Stewart. But that is hard to avoid . . .

"The title of this script doesn't come over. And I have often wished that our titles might conform to the stylized pattern of all my short stories, which deliberately follow the formula, you may have noticed, of 'The Adjective Noun,' almost as a trademark (except when they are 'The Man Who . . .')."[1]

The book was first published in 1969 by the Doubleday Crime Club. By 11 June the following year they'd sold 5,713 copies and it went out of print on 1 July that year. A UK edition was published on 18 May 1970.

---

1 *The Saint on TV*, Ian Dickerson (Hirst Publishing, 2011)

A Dutch edition, *De Saint en de kunstminnaars*, was published in 1969 but remains the only foreign-language translation to date.

ABOUT THE AUTHOR

*I'm mad enough to believe in romance. And I'm sick and
tired of this age—tired of the miserable little mildewed
things that people racked their brains about, and wrote
books about, and called life. I wanted something more
elementary and honest—battle, murder, sudden death, with
plenty of good beer and damsels in distress, and a complete
callousness about blipping the ungodly over the beezer. It
mayn't be life as we know it, but it ought to be.*

—Leslie Charteris in a 1935 BBC radio interview

Leslie Charteris was born Leslie Charles Bowyer-Yin in Singapore on
12 May 1907.

He was the son of a Chinese doctor and his English wife, who'd
met in London a few years earlier. Young Leslie found friends hard to
come by in colonial Singapore. The English children had been told not
to play with Eurasians, and the Chinese children had been told not to
play with Europeans. Leslie was caught in between and took refuge in
reading.

"I read a great many good books and enjoyed them because
nobody had told me that they were classics. I also read a great many
bad books which nobody told me not to read . . . I read a great many

popular scientific articles and acquired from them an astonishing amount of general knowledge before I discovered that this acquisition was supposed to be a chore."[1]

One of his favourite things to read was a magazine called *Chums*. "The Best and Brightest Paper for Boys" (if you believe the adverts) was a monthly paper full of swashbuckling adventure stories aimed at boys, encouraging them to be honourable and moral and perhaps even "upright citizens with furled umbrellas."[2] Undoubtedly these types of stories would influence his later work.

When his parents split up shortly after the end of World War I, Charteris accompanied his mother and brother back to England, where he was sent to Rossall School in Fleetwood, Lancashire. Rossall was then a very stereotypical English public school, and it struggled to cope with this multilingual mixed-race boy just into his teens who'd already seen more of the world than many of his peers would see in their lifetimes. He was an outsider.

He left Rossall in 1924. Keen to pursue a creative career, he decided to study art in Paris—after all, that was where the great artists went—but soon found that the life of a literally starving artist didn't appeal. He continued writing, firing off speculative stories to magazines, and it was the sale of a short story to *Windsor Magazine* that saved him from penury.

He returned to London in 1925, as his parents—particularly his father—wanted him to become a lawyer, and he was sent to study law at Cambridge University. In the mid-1920s, Cambridge was full of Bright Young Things—aristocrats and bohemians somewhat typified in the Evelyn Waugh novel *Vile Bodies*—and again the mixed-race Bowyer-Yin found that he didn't fit in. He was an outsider who preferred to make his own way in the world and wasn't one of the privileged upper class. It didn't help that he found his studies boring and decided it was more fun contemplating ways to circumvent the law. This inspired him to write a novel, and when publishers Ward Lock & Co. offered him a three-book deal on the strength of it, he abandoned his studies to pursue a writing career.

When his father learnt of this, he was not impressed, as he considered writers to be "rogues and vagabonds." Charteris would later recall that "I wanted to be a writer, he wanted me to become a lawyer. I was stubborn, he said I would end up in the gutter. So I left home. Later on, when I had a little success, we were reconciled by letter, but I never saw him again."[3]

X Esquire, his first novel, appeared in April 1927. The lead character, X Esquire, is a mysterious hero, hunting down and killing the businessmen trying to wipe out Britain by distributing quantities of free poisoned cigarettes. His second novel, *The White Rider*, was published the following spring, and in one memorable scene shows the hero chasing after his damsel in distress, only for him to overtake the villains, leap into their car . . . and promptly faint.

These two plot highlights may go some way to explaining Charteris's comment on *Meet—the Tiger!*, published in September 1928, that "it was only the third book I'd written, and the best, I would say, for it was that the first two were even worse."[4]

Twenty-one-year-old authors are naturally self-critical. Despite reasonably good reviews, the Saint didn't set the world on fire, and Charteris moved on to a new hero for his next book. This was *The Bandit*, an adventure story featuring Ramon Francisco De Castilla y Espronceda Manrique, published in the summer of 1929 after its serialisation in the *Empire News*, a now long-forgotten Sunday newspaper. But sales of *The Bandit* were less than impressive, and Charteris began to question his choice of career. It was all very well writing—but if nobody wants to read what you write, what's the point?

"I had to succeed, because before me loomed the only alternative, the dreadful penalty of failure . . . the routine office hours, the five-day week . . . the lethal assimilation into the ranks of honest, hard-working, conformist, God-fearing pillars of the community."[5]

However his fortunes—and the Saint's—were about to change. In late 1928, Leslie had met Monty Haydon, a London-based editor who was looking for writers to pen stories for his new paper, *The Thriller*—"The Paper with a Thousand Thrills." Charteris later recalled that "he said he was starting a new magazine, had read one of my books and would like some stories from me. I couldn't have been more grateful, both from the point of view of vanity and finance!"[6]

The paper launched in early 1929, and Leslie's first work, "The Story of a Dead Man," featuring Jimmy Traill, appeared in issue 4 (published on 2 March 1929). That was followed just over a month later with "The Secret of Beacon Inn," starring Rameses "Pip" Smith. At the same time, Leslie finished writing another non-Saint novel, *Daredevil*, which would be published in late 1929. Storm Arden was the hero; more notably, the book saw the first introduction of a Scotland Yard inspector by the name of Claud Eustace Teal.

The Saint returned in the thirteenth issue of *The Thriller*. The byline proclaimed that the tale was "A Thrilling Complete Story of the Underworld"; the title was "The Five Kings," and it actually featured Four Kings and a Joker. Simon Templar, of course, was the Joker.

Charteris spent the rest of 1929 telling the adventures of the Five Kings in five subsequent *The Thriller* stories. "It was very hard work, for the pay was lousy, but Monty Haydon was a brilliant and stimulating editor, full of ideas. While he didn't actually help shape the Saint as a character, he did suggest story lines. He would take me out to lunch and say, 'What are you going to write about next?' I'd often say I was damned if I knew. And Monty would say, 'Well, I was reading something the other day . . .' He had a fund of ideas and we would talk them over, and then I would go away and write a story. He was a great creative editor."[7]

Charteris would have one more attempt at writing about a hero other than Simon Templar, in three novelettes published in *The Thriller* in early 1930, but he swiftly returned to the Saint. This was partly due to his self-confessed laziness—he wanted to write more stories for *The Thriller* and other magazines, and creating a new hero for every story was hard work—but mainly due to feedback from Monty Haydon. It seemed people wanted to read more adventures of the Saint . . .

Charteris would contribute over forty stories to *The Thriller* throughout the 1930s. Shortly after their debut, he persuaded publisher Hodder & Stoughton that if he collected some of these stories and rewrote them a little, they could publish them as a Saint book. *Enter the Saint* was first published in August 1930, and the reaction was good enough for the publishers to bring out another collection. And another . . .

Of the twenty Saint books published in the 1930s, almost all have their origins in those magazine stories.

Why was the Saint so popular throughout the decade? Aside from the charm and ability of Charteris's storytelling, the stories, particularly those published in the first half of the '30s, are full of energy and joie de vivre. With economic depression rampant throughout the period, the public at large seemed to want some escapism.

And Simon Templar's appeal was wide-ranging: he wasn't an upper-class hero like so many of the period. With no obvious background and no attachment to the Old School Tie, no friends in high places who could provide a get-out-of-jail-free card, the Saint was uniquely classless. Not unlike his creator.

Throughout Leslie's formative years, his heritage had been an issue. In his early days in Singapore, during his time at school, at Cambridge University or even just in everyday life, he couldn't avoid the fact that for many people his mixed parentage was a problem. He would later tell a story of how he was chased up the road by a stick-waving typical

English gent who took offence to his daughter being escorted around town by a foreigner.

Like the Saint, he was an outsider. And although he had spent a significant portion of his formative years in England, he couldn't settle.

As a young boy he had read of an America "peopled largely by Indians, and characters in fringed buckskin jackets who fought nobly against them. I spent a great deal of time day-dreaming about a visit to this prodigious and exciting country."[8]

It was time to realise this wish. Charteris and his first wife, Pauline, whom he'd met in London when they were both teenagers and married in 1931, set sail for the States in late 1932; the Saint had already made his debut in America courtesy of the publisher Doubleday. Charteris and his wife found a New York still experiencing the tail end of Prohibition, and times were tough at first. Despite sales to *The American Magazine* and others, it wasn't until a chance meeting with writer turned Hollywood executive Bartlett McCormack in their favourite speakeasy that Charteris's career stepped up a gear.

Soon Charteris was in Hollywood, working on what would become the 1933 movie *Midnight Club*. However, Hollywood's treatment of writers wasn't to Charteris's taste, and he began to yearn for home. Within a few months, he returned to the UK and began writing more Saint stories for Monty Haydon and Bill McElroy.

He also rewrote a story he'd sketched out whilst in the States, a version of which had been published in *The American Magazine* in September 1934. This new novel, *The Saint in New York*, published in 1935, was a significant advance for the Saint and Leslie Charteris. Gone were the high jinks and the badinage. The youthful exuberance evident in the Saint's early adventures had evolved into something a little darker, a little more hard-boiled. It was the next stage in development for the author and his creation, and readers loved it. It became a bestseller on both sides of the Atlantic.

Having spent his formative years in places as far apart as Singapore and England, with substantial travel in between, it should be no surprise that Leslie had a serious case of wanderlust. With a bestseller under his belt, he now had the means to see more of the world.

Nineteen thirty-six found him in Tenerife, researching another Saint adventure alongside translating the biography of Juan Belmonte, a well-known Spanish matador. Estranged for several months, Leslie and Pauline divorced in 1937. The following year, Leslie married an American, Barbara Meyer, who'd accompanied him to Tenerife. In early 1938, Charteris and his new bride set off in a trailer of his own design and spent eighteen months travelling round America and Canada.

The Saint in New York had reminded Hollywood of Charteris's talents, and film rights to the novel were sold prior to publication in 1935. Although the proposed 1935 film production was rejected by the Hays Office for its violent content, RKO's eventual 1938 production persuaded Charteris to try his luck once more in Hollywood.

New opportunities had opened up, and throughout the 1940s the Saint appeared not only in books and movies but in a newspaper strip, a comic-book series, and on radio.

Anyone wishing to adapt the character in any medium found a stern taskmaster in Charteris. He was never completely satisfied, nor was he shy of showing his displeasure. He did, however, ensure that copyright in any Saint adventure belonged to him, even if scripted by another writer—a contractual obligation that he was to insist on throughout his career.

Charteris was soon spread thin, overseeing movies, comics, newspapers, and radio versions of his creation, and this, along with his self-proclaimed laziness, meant that Saint books were becoming fewer and further between. However, he still enjoyed his creation: in 1941 he indulged himself in a spot of fun by playing the Saint—complete with monocle and moustache—in a photo story in *Life* magazine.

In July 1944, he started collaborating under a pseudonym on Sherlock Holmes radio scripts, subsequently writing more adventures for Holmes than Conan Doyle. Not all his ventures were successful—a screenplay he was hired to write for Deanna Durbin, "Lady on a Train," took him a year and ultimately bore little resemblance to the finished film. In the mid-1940s, Charteris successfully sued RKO Pictures for unfair competition after they launched a new series of films starring George Sanders as a debonair crime fighter known as the Falcon. But he kept faith with his original character, and the Saint novels continued to adapt to the times. The transatlantic Saint evolved into something of a private operator, working for the mysterious Hamilton and becoming, not unlike his creator, a world traveller, finding that adventure would seek him out.

"I have never been able to see why a fictional character should not grow up, mature, and develop, the same as anyone else. The same, if you like, as his biographer. The only adequate reason is that—so far as I know—no other fictional character in modern times has survived a sufficient number of years for these changes to be clearly observable. I must confess that a lot of my own selfish pleasure in the Saint has been in watching him grow up."[9]

Charteris maintained his love of travel and was soon to be found sailing round the West Indies with his good friend Gregory Peck. His forays abroad gave him even more material, and he began to write true-crime articles, as well as an occasional column in *Gourmet* magazine.

By the early '50s, Charteris himself was feeling strained. He'd divorced his second wife in 1943 and got together with a New York radio and nightclub singer called Betty Bryant Borst, whom he married in late 1943. That relationship had fallen apart acrimoniously towards the end of the decade, and he roamed the globe restlessly, rarely in one place for longer than a couple of months. He continued to maintain a firm grip on the exploitation of the Saint in various media but was writing little himself. The Saint had become an industry, and Charteris couldn't keep up. He began thinking seriously about an early retirement. Then in 1951 he met a young actress called Audrey Long when they became next-door neighbours in Hollywood. Within a year they had married, a union that was to last the rest of Leslie's life. He attacked life with a new vitality. They travelled—Nassau was a favoured escape spot—and he wrote. He struck an agreement with *The New York Herald Tribune* for a Saint comic strip, which would appear daily and be written by Charteris himself. The strip ran for thirteen years, with Charteris sending in his handwritten story lines from wherever he happened to be, relying on mail services around the world to continue the Saint's adventures. New Saint books began to appear, and Charteris reached a height of productivity not seen since his days as a struggling author trying to establish himself. As Leslie and Audrey travelled, so did the Saint, visiting locations just after his creator had been there.

By 1953 the Saint had already enjoyed twenty-five years of success, and *The Saint Detective Magazine* was launched. Charteris had become adept at exploiting his creation to the full, mixing new stories with repackaged older stories, sometimes rewritten, sometimes mixed up in "new" anthologies, sometimes adapted from radio scripts previously written by other writers.

Charteris had been approached several times over the years for television rights in the Saint and had expended much time and effort during the 1950s trying to get the Saint on TV, even going so far as to write sample scripts himself, but it wasn't to be. He finally agreed a deal in autumn 1961 with English film producers Robert S. Baker and Monty Berman. The first episode of *The Saint* television series, starring Roger Moore, went into production in June 1962. The series was an immediate success, though Charteris himself had his reservations. It reached second place in the ratings, but he commented that "in that distinction it was topped by wrestling, which only suggested to me that the competition may not have been so hot; but producers are generally cast in a less modest mould." He resented the implication that the TV series had finally made a success of the Saint after twenty-five years of literary obscurity.

As long as the series lasted, Charteris was not shy about voicing his criticisms both in public and in a constant stream of memos to the producers. "Regular followers of the Saint saga . . . must have noticed that I am almost incapable of simply writing a story and shutting up."[10] Nor was he shy about exploiting this new market by agreeing to a series of tie-in novelisations ghosted by other writers, which he would then rewrite before publication.

Charteris mellowed as the series developed and found elements to praise too. He developed a close friendship with producer Robert S. Baker, which would last until Charteris's death.

In the early '60s, on one of their frequent trips to England, Leslie and Audrey bought a house in Surrey, which became their permanent base. He explored the possibility of a Saint musical and began writing some of it himself.

Charteris no longer needed to work. Now in his sixties, he supervised the Saint from a distance whilst continuing to travel and indulge himself. He and Audrey made seasonal excursions to Ireland and the south of France, where they had residences. He began to write poetry and devised a new universal sign language, Paleneo, based on notes and symbols he used in his diaries. Once Paleneo was released, he decided enough was enough and announced, again, his retirement. This time he meant it.

The Saint continued regardless—there was a long-running Swedish comic strip, and new novels with other writers doing the bulk of the work were complemented in the 1970s with Bob Baker's revival of the TV series, *Return of the Saint*.

Ill-health began to take its toll. By the early 1980s, although he continued a healthy correspondence with the outside world, Charteris felt unable to keep up with the collaborative Saint books and pulled the plug on them.

To entertain himself, Leslie took to "trying to beat the bookies in predicting the relative speed of horses," a hobby which resulted in several of his local betting shops refusing to take "predictions" from him, as he was too successful for their liking.

He still received requests to publish his work abroad but had become completely cynical about further attempts to revive the Saint. A new Saint magazine only lasted three issues, and two TV productions—*The Saint in Manhattan*, with Tom Selleck look-alike Andrew Clarke, and *The Saint*, with Simon Dutton—left him bitterly disappointed. "I fully expect this series to lay eggs everywhere . . . the only satisfaction I have is in looking at my bank balance."[11]

In the early 1990s, Hollywood producers Robert Evans and William J. Macdonald approached him and made a deal for the Saint to return to cinema screens. Charteris still took great care of the Saint's reputation and wrote an outline entitled *The Return of the Saint* in which an older Saint would meet the son he didn't know he had.

Much of his time in his last few years was taken up with the movie. Several scripts were submitted to him—each moving further and further away from his original concept—but the screenwriter from 1940s Hollywood was thoroughly disheartened by the Hollywood of the '90s: "There is still no plot, no real story, no characterisations, no personal interaction, nothing but endless frantic violence . . ." Besides, with producer Bill Macdonald hitting the headlines for the most un-Saintly reasons, he was to add, "How can Bill Macdonald concentrate on my Saint movie when he has Sharon Stone in his bed?"

The Crime Writers' Association of Great Britain presented Leslie with a Lifetime Achievement award in 1992 in a special ceremony at the

House of Lords. Never one for associations and awards, and although visibly unwell, Leslie accepted the award with grace and humour ("I am now only waiting to be carbon-dated," he joked). He suffered a slight stroke in his final weeks, which did not prevent him from dining out locally with family and friends, before he finally passed away at the age of 85 on 15 April 1993.

His death severed one of the final links with the classic thriller genre of the 1930s and 1940s, but he left behind a legacy of nearly one hundred books, countless short stories, and TV, film, radio, and comic-strip adaptations of his work which will endure for generations to come.

> *I was always sure that there was a solid place in escape literature for a rambunctious adventurer such as I dreamed up in my youth, who really believed in the old-fashioned romantic ideals and was prepared to lay everything on the line to bring them to life. A joyous exuberance that could not find its fulfilment in pinball machines and pot. I had what may now seem a mad desire to spread the belief that there were worse, and wickeder, nut cases than Don Quixote.*
>
> *Even now, half a century later, when I should be old enough to know better, I still cling to that belief. That there will always be a public for the old-style hero, who had a clear idea of justice, and a more than technical approach to love, and the ability to have some fun with his crusades.*[12]

---

1 *A Letter from the Saint*, 30 August 1946
2 "The Last Word," *The First Saint Omnibus*, Doubleday Crime Club, 1939
3 *The Straits Times*, 29 June 1958, page 9

4 Introduction by Charteris to the September 1980 paperback reprint of *Meet—the Tiger!* (Charter), the last ever print edition.

5 *The Saint: A Complete History*, by Burl Barer (McFarland, 1993)

6 PR material from the 1970s series *Return of the Saint*

7 From "Return of the Saint: Comprehensive Information" issued to help publicise the 1970s TV show

8 *A Letter from the Saint*, 26 July 1946

9 Introduction to "The Million Pound Day," in *The First Saint Omnibus*

10 *A Letter from the Saint*, 12 April 1946

11 Letter from LC to sometime Saint collaborator Peter Bloxsom, 2 August 1989

12 Introduction by Charteris to the September 1980 paperback reprint of *Meet—the Tiger!* (Charter).

WATCH FOR THE SIGN

OF THE SAINT!

THE SAINT CLUB

*And so, my friends, dear bookworms, most noble fellow
drinkers, frustrated burglars, affronted policemen, upright
citizens with furled umbrellas and secret buccaneering
dreams that seems to be very nearly all for now. It has been
nice having you with us, and we hope you will come again,
not once, but many times.*

*Only because of our great love for you, we would like
to take this parting opportunity of mentioning one small
matter which we have very much at heart . . .*

—*Leslie Charteris,* The First Saint Omnibus *(1939)*

Leslie Charteris founded The Saint Club in 1936 with the aim of
providing a constructive fanbase for Saint devotees. Before the War, it
donated profits to a London hospital where, for several years, a Saint
ward was maintained. With the nationalisation of hospitals, profits
were, for many years, donated to the Arbour Youth Centre in Stepney,
London.

In the twenty-first century, we've carried on this tradition but have
also donated to the Red Cross and a number of different children's
charities.

The club acts as a focal point for anyone interested in the adventures of Leslie Charteris and the work of Simon Templar, and offers merchandise that includes DVDs of the old TV series and various Saint-related publications, through to its own exclusive range of notepaper, pin badges, and polo shirts. All profits are donated to charity. The club also maintains two popular websites and supports many more Saint-related sites.

After Leslie Charteris's death, the club recruited three new vice-presidents—Roger Moore, Ian Ogilvy, and Simon Dutton have all pledged their support, whilst Audrey and Patricia Charteris have been retained as Saints-in-Chief. But some things do not change, for the back of the membership card still mischievously proclaims that . . .

The bearer of this card is probably a person of hideous antecedents and low moral character, and upon apprehension for any cause should be immediately released in order to save other prisoners from contamination.

To join . . .

Membership costs £3.50 (or US$7) per year, or £30 (US$60) for life. Find us online at www.lesliecharteris.com for full details.

Made in the USA
Monee, IL
15 July 2020